"Bang Bang," The Joker Said As He Pulled The Trigger.

The Joker had pressed the cold muzzle of the revolver against Winter's forehead. The hammer clicked on empty cylinders.

"What are you doing to me?" Winter whispered.

"To whom?" the Joker replied graciously. "You don't exist anymore, do you? As I recall it, you are no longer with us." He stepped back and waved at Dr. Andrews, who now stood beside him. "We do have a new guest, however."

The doctor must have walked in while Winter had his eyes closed. Any small hope Winter had always vanished the instant the doctor arrived.

"Doctor," the Joker asked, "If you will give him the injection?"

"Gladly." The doctor stepped forward.

"From this moment forward," the doctor remarked pleasantly as he grabbed Winter's forearm, "you are Batman."

THE BATMAN MURDERS

ALSO BY
CRAIG SHAW GARDNER

BATMAN

Published by
WARNER BOOKS

THE BATMAN MURDERS

CRAIG SHAW GARDNER

WARNER BOOKS

A Time Warner Company

WARNER BOOKS EDITION

Copyright © 1990 by DC Comics, Inc.
All rights reserved. The stories, characters, and incidents featured in this
publication are entirely fictional. All characters, their distinctive
likenesses, and all related indicia are trademarks of DC Comics, Inc.

Cover illustration by Dave Dorman

Warner Books, Inc.
666 Fifth Avenue
New York, N.Y. 10103

 A Time Warner Company

Printed in the United States of America

First Printing: October, 1990

10 9 8 7 6 5 4 3 2 1

THE
BATMAN
MURDERS

PROLOGUE

*The man sat in the dark room, the absolutely dark room.
There was no sound here either, except the sound that
issued from the man's lips.*

Why, then, was the man laughing?

There was no moon in Gotham City. The steaming August day had brought heavy clouds, but no rain. The dark clouds hung there like a blanket pressing the heat onto the sweltering streets below. Darkness and heat, a bad combination. It brought crime into the city like a roach, scurrying from its hole and looking to see what it could devour in the absence of light.

There was no moon in Gotham City. The humid air seemed to dull the streetlights and neon, their glow barely filtering to the street. Sounds, though, were everywhere —music, arguments, laughter, screams, all fighting with one another on the sleepless streets, the million voices of the city rising and falling with a rhythm to match the waves down by Gotham harbor.

Some listened for the music.

One man listened for the screams.

There was no moon in Gotham City, and darkness bred all sorts of things.

But darkness had another friend. A shadow moved on the rooftops, on a night when there were no shadows. And this shadow leaned over the edge to watch his prey.

There were three of them in the alleyway below, three common criminals, about to break into the First Gotham Bank. Their voices carried in the still, heavy air, and he heard all their plans, but he had to wait for them to make their move. First, they would commit their crime. Then they would meet the Batman.

Still, he wished they would get on with it. Maybe it was something about the night, but it was very difficult to wait for action. The cape was heavy on his back, the fabric of his uniform damp against his skin. Why was he worried? The three below were no match for him.

They started at last, all three of them moving to the side entrance of the bank. Maybe they had to wait for a prearranged time. There was probably a fourth man, a driver, who would show up when they'd finished the job. They had used glass cutters to cut a small hole in the glass on the side door, and a thermite lance to burn out the old lock so that they could just push the door in with the kick of a boot. It looked like they had found the weakest point in the old bank building. All three walked quickly inside. There was no alarm. These guys were professional enough to take care of that.

But it was time for Batman to get to work, too.

He tugged one more time on the hook he'd set on the chimney. It would hold. The bank robbers below had spent so long waiting that he'd had plenty of time to find the best place to secure his line. He stepped to the edge of the roof, then jumped, gliding down on the rope.

Something was wrong. The building was higher than he thought. The angle was too great, he was going too fast. He landed on the ground with a jolt, jarring his left leg. It was a foolish mistake. He'd been out of action too long, too eager for the hunt. He had to calm himself, become centered. He'd have a fight on his hands soon enough.

He took a step, and felt a pain in his left leg. He must have slightly twisted his ankle. His mistake would cost him more than he thought. Still, there was nothing to do but ignore it and go on.

He walked quickly to the side entrance. The criminals had left the door open four or five inches, enough so somebody would notice. Maybe they weren't as professional as he had thought. He knew there was a night watchman in this place. If he could, he should get to the crooks before they got to the watchman. Sweeny, that was the watchman's name. Sometimes even Batman was amazed by all that he knew.

The door opened silently, and Batman crept inside, staying in shadow. He was on the main business floor of the bank, the one with all the teller's cages and loan officer's desks. One of the three criminals was across the room, working on the upstairs vault. There was no sign of the others, but the door that led to the basement levels was wide open. That's where the real money would be, down in the large vault the bank used to supply all its branches.

There were safe deposit boxes down there, too, full of the valuables of hundreds of the bank's customers. There was no sign of Sweeny, either. He hoped he wasn't too late.

Batman had to move fast, before the robbers got too far. He'd take out the one up here first. He reached down to his belt and pulled out a modified boomerang with an attached nylon line. A simple toss, and the boomerang cord would wind itself around the robber long enough for Batman to knock him cold.

He threw as he stepped forward onto his left foot. He grunted as pain shot up his leg. His toss had gone wide. The boomerang clattered behind the teller's cages.

"Wha—" The crook looked up from where he had been concentrating on the lock. He stood and took a couple of steps toward the cages.

Trouble. Batman had to take out the guy now, before he could warn the others. He moved toward the vault as fast as his injured ankle would let him. The ankle didn't allow him to move as quietly as he would like, either. He could hear the sound of his boots on the floor as he ran. He was breathing heavily by the time he reached the crook. The robber turned around, and Batman put all he had behind a single punch.

The crook yelled as he saw the fist, just before Batman knocked him senseless. One down, but Batman might have lost the element of surprise.

He hurried to the door leading downstairs. There was an old, circular, wrought-iron stairs in the alcove here, dating back from when the bank was built, close to a hundred years ago. He knew, before he even looked down, that the stairs led to three levels of basement—a basement where the bank's founding fathers thought that vaults and safe deposit boxes would be safer from robbers. There was a service elevator back here, too. It was Batman's business to know about banks, and that knowledge would serve him well now. It was Batman's business to know about every aspect of crime.

The elevator opened as he walked through the doorway from the bank. There was no place for him to run. He braced himself to fight.

The man inside the elevator stared at him openmouthed. It was the night watchman.

"Sweeny?" he called softly.

"Batman?" the watchman replied incredulously, as if he couldn't believe his eyes.

"Sweeny, what's happening?" he demanded.

Sweeny shook his head. "Happening?" he asked. "I just began my two A.M. rounds. Is something wrong?"

Somehow, Batman realized, the watchman has missed the criminals—and luckily for Sweeny, the criminals had missed him, too.

"Don't worry," he told the watchman. "I'll take care of it."

Batman took a step toward the elevator. The pain in his left leg was even worse—he shouldn't have run on it. His knee wanted to buckle underneath him. He leaned forward, trying to catch his breath.

A gun went off behind him. He heard the whine of a bullet, close by his ear. The crooks had found him. If he hadn't leaned forward, the bullet would have caught him in the back.

"Keep out of the way!" he barked to the watchman.

He turned to face the robbers, two of them, with guns drawn. Both of them were smiling. He'd show them there was nothing to smile about. He'd teach them to fear the Batman.

"Who do you think you're trying to fool?" Sweeny called out behind him. What was the watchman talking about?

Somebody shoved him in the back; somebody who had to be Sweeny. Batman realized the watchman must be working with the bank robbers, making it an inside job. Not Sweeny. He'd been with the bank for almost twenty years.

Batman tried to stop himself from falling, but his leg collapsed underneath him, and he toppled over the railing, three long stories down.

He had one last thought as he fell:

Batman couldn't die, could he?

PART I

One Batman
Too Many

1

He had slept poorly the night before. He'd had the dream again.

But now Bruce Wayne was instantly awake.

"Sir?" Alfred had had that tone in his voice when he had handed him the morning paper. "Something of interest."

Bruce always marveled at how much import his butler could put in four words. Alfred was always so calm, so unruffled, that a lifted eyebrow could mean he was about to inform his employer of the most dire catastrophe imaginable. And when he raised the pitch of his voice slightly at the end of the sentence as he just had, well, things were really serious.

Bruce didn't realize how serious they were until he opened to the headline. It ran across the entire top of *The Gotham Globe*, in 128-point type.

THE BATMAN MURDER?
Bizarre Death of Leading Gotham Banker
Dressed as Caped Crusader
While First Gotham Robbed of Millions
Police Unable to Rule Out Suicide

Below that were two photos, side by side, the one on the left a well-lit, professional studio photo of a prosperous-looking, portly gentleman in his middle fifties, with the caption: First Gotham Bank Vice President Milton T. Cranshaw.

The larger photo on the right wasn't well lit at all. It showed, in fuzzy black-and-white, an overweight man who had been stuffed into a badly sewn Batman costume. He was stretched out on what Bruce guessed was an inlaid tile floor. From the unnatural position of the man's arms and legs, Bruce could tell there had been a number of broken bones.

The caption below this photograph read: The late Cranshaw in Batman suit, apparently killed by fifty-foot fall.

Alfred placed Bruce's usual breakfast of grapefruit, cereal, and dry toast in front of him.

"Shall I call the commissioner?"

Bruce shook his head. "Commissioner Gordon is attending the police convention in Kansas City. He should be back this evening around five."

"I see," the butler replied. "Mr. Winter is running the show?"

Alfred sighed as Bruce nodded his head. His old friend knew as well as Bruce did that it wasn't worth trying to get any cooperation out of Steven Winter.

Bruce frowned back at the paper. If Gordon had been

around, the commissioner would have called Batman in right away rather than letting him read about the incident in the morning paper. A man found dead in a Batman uniform—what could it mean? As careful as the police might be about maintaining the integrity of the scene of the crime, the longer it took Batman to examine the evidence, the more chance there might be that something, perhaps a vital clue—a few hairs carried away on a policeman's shoe, a whiff of gas sucked off by the air-conditioning system—would be lost.

Maybe, Bruce thought, he was overreacting because the dead man was dressed the way he was. He had to be careful not to overreact. He knew he had been pushing himself too hard lately. Still, still—

THE BATMAN MURDER, the headline read. He looked again at the photo of the overweight banker, so strange-looking the way he was stuffed into the homemade Batman costume.

He supposed there could be any number of explanations for this so-called bizarre death. Maybe this middle-aged businessman, Cranshaw, had somehow fixated on Batman. Cranshaw could have even arranged the robbery personally, so that he could then delude himself into believing he was the costumed crime fighter who would stop that robbery. Realizing what he had done, the banker could even have thrown himself to his death.

Sometimes people identified too strongly with the famous—it was one of the prices of notoriety, especially when so many considered you to be a hero. Batman sometimes filled much too large a hole in people's lives.

Why, then, did Bruce take this so personally? Every time he looked at the fat body in the crude suit, he felt as though someone was criticizing Bruce's life; thumbing his nose at anybody who put on a costume disguise to fight crime in Gotham City.

Bruce put down the paper. A good detective never assumed anything until he had gained as much information as he could gather. He needed to look at the scene of the crime. There must be some way Batman could get Winter to see that!

He popped a couple of vitamins in his mouth and drank his orange juice. He was too agitated at the moment to eat anything else.

"Alfred?" he called to his butler. "Clear this away, would you? I have to go for a ride."

"Want to buy a flower, mister?"

Special Mayoral Assistant Steven Winter ignored the kid pushing the daisy in his face and quickly climbed the steps to Gotham City Hall. Commissioner Gordon's absence gave him the perfect opportunity to study the real structure of the Gotham police force without interference.

If there was one thing that Winter had learned from the mayor, it was that *everything* was politics, and the police were no exception. The mayor was more interested in the structure underneath the commissioner. That was Winter's specialty: finding out who really ran the show in the various city departments he "oversaw."

As far as the police were concerned, Winter had already discovered there wasn't much power sharing near the top. Gordon wasn't the sort to delegate much in the way of real responsibility. Gordon's second-in-command, John W. O'Neal, was a year away from his pension, and didn't want anything (decision making included) interfering with his happy retirement. That made Winter's job even easier, since—whatever inquiries he might make—O'Neal was guaranteed to look the other way.

So Winter searched for the real centers of influence in the police force: certain individuals, such as Captain Grant down in Vice, and groups, such as the elite S.W.A.T. team Gordon had had trained at the army facility, that the rest of the officers on the police looked up to. And once Winter found the real leaders and opinion makers, it would be amazing how quickly the mayor would choose to lavish a little extra attention here, and grant a special favor or two there, so that, when the time came, the mayor could ask for a favor or two of his own.

It wasn't that Commissioner Gordon was necessarily doing a bad job. But a city the size and complexity of Gotham had special needs, and the mayor had his own thoughts on law and order. Commissioner Gordon had been in office a long time; he had become set in his ways, sometimes treating criminals with a total disregard for public opinion, but—most of all according to the mayor—depending far too much on that masked vigilante, Batman.

What the mayor wanted, and therefore the mayor's assistant wanted, was a police commissioner who thought like the mayor; ideally, a man who had been put in office by that mayor. Officially, Winter was spending a month in the commissioner's office "observing." However, he was really here to make sure that the police rank and file saw things the mayor's way, so that the next time elections rolled around, it would be that much easier for the mayor's man to become the new commissioner.

Winter nodded pleasantly at his fellow workers as he marched down the long corridor to his temporary quarters.

Many nodded back. Some ignored him, too busy with their overworked lives to even think about who he was, much less what he was trying to do.

He stepped into the suite of rooms that held the offices of the commissioner and his aides. Every time he walked in here, he realized again that he hadn't been totally successful in camouflaging his true intentions. He could see it in the office workers here—Gordon's family, he liked to call them—who regarded him with suspicion and, in the case of Gordon's secretary, Ms. Davis, open hostility.

"Oh, Mr. Winter," Davis's voice called from over by the file cabinet. He turned toward her with his best public smile, ready for her frown and withering gaze.

"I'm so glad you're here," Ms. Davis continued. She actually looked happy to see him. Winter almost lost his own smile. Something must be very wrong here.

"Phone for you, sir." She pointed at the red receiver resting on her desk. "It's—um—it's Batman."

She was almost laughing by now. Winter cleared his throat to cover his annoyance. How could she know how much he disliked the vigilante crime fighter? Still, he had been expecting this call since two A.M. last night. This was the sort of thing the mayor paid him for. He might as well get it over with.

"Thank you, Ms. Davis," he replied, keeping his voice as light as possible. "I'll get it in my office."

He walked quickly to the small, enclosed cubicle at the back of the suite and closed the door behind him. He gave himself a moment to take a deep breath, then picked up the phone.

"Steve Winter here. So nice to hear from you, Batman."

"Winter?" the voice on the phone demanded. "Why wasn't I informed of last night's incident at the First Gotham Bank?"

Winter had had plenty of experience handling anger, even from a guy who wore a bat costume. "I'm sorry," Winter answered smoothly, "but I wasn't in a position to divulge any details. That was privileged police information."

"Haven't I worked long enough with the police—" The angry voice stopped and was replaced by a much calmer tone. "Don't you think that due to the circumstances involved I might be able to shed some light on the situation?"

Winter paused for a second. He actually found Batman's neutral, emotionless tone much more disquieting than his anger. "Well," he answered rapidly, with as much cheer as he could muster, "now that you mention it, I'm sure you have a point, and when Commissioner Gordon returns, I'll be glad to bring up your concerns at my first opportunity."

"First opportunity?" Batman's voice was still, somehow, as calm as the grave. "Valuable evidence could be lost while you are—"

Winter decided he didn't want to hear any more of this. "So nice to talk to you, Batman. I'm afraid, though, in the commissioner's absence, there are other matters that must take priority. We must get a chance to talk at some greater length. I assure you that I will keep in touch."

He hung up the phone. Nobody, not even Batman, told Steven Winter what to do. Especially today, with all the calls and contacts he wanted to make. After all, Commissioner Gordon would be back here at day's end, and Winter would have to be far more circumspect.

He opened the door to his office. There was Assistant Commissioner O'Neal, his hands resting over his ample stomach, at his usual position by the water cooler.

"Johnny?" Winter called. "Can I talk to you for a minute?"

Ms. Davis looked up from where she was sorting and stapling papers at her desk. Winter noticed that her disapproving frown was back. She was probably hoping that after the call from Batman, he would crawl, sniveling, from the office, never to be seen again.

"Oh, sure, Steve!" O'Neal waved his paper cup at the mayor's assistant. "Just wetting my whistle before I get back to work!" He strode, slowly but purposefully, across the room. "What can I do for you today?"

"More of the same," Winter assured him.

O'Neal grinned. "Picking my brain, are you? Getting at my thirty-five years of police work?"

"You're a national resource, Johnny," Winter assured him. He stepped back into his office. "I need to know a bit more about the precinct chiefs." He pulled a cigarette from the pack on his desk, then waved toward the chair on the side of the desk. "Would you like to sit down?"

O'Neal shook his head as he leaned heavily against the metal frame of Winter's door. "That's all right. This doorway looks like it could use some propping up. Now what can I really do for you?"

Winter lit his cigarette and inhaled deeply. "I need to hear a couple of your stories, Johnny. You know I'm interested in the way things really work—"

Winter paused as he heard an animated conversation drift in from the outer office. O'Neal turned his head to see what was happening. When he looked back at Winter, he was no longer smiling.

"Excuse me," O'Neal murmured. "I have to get back to my paperwork." He turned and walked away, much more quickly than usual.

"Johnny?" Winter called, but the chubby assistant commissioner was gone.

"Good to see you," O'Neal said to someone in the outer office.

O'Neal's place in the doorway was taken by a shape that seemed to fill the entire door frame. Winter almost swallowed his cigarette.

It was Batman.

Winter stubbed out his cigarette in the ashtray at the corner of his desk and did his best to look levelly at the figure in the doorway. This was the first time Winter had ever seen him this close, the first time he had ever been watched by the man's steel-grey eyes.

"Um—" he began. "Can I help you?"

The visible half of Batman's face smiled. "We were looking for an opportunity to get together," he spoke in that all-too-calm voice. "You said you wanted to talk at some greater length."

So Batman was trying to force the issue. Well, Steve Winter would not be intimidated. Still, he couldn't help but wonder how Batman had gotten here so quickly. Where had he phoned from? Down the hall?

"Really, Batman," Winter began. His gaze drifted down from the man's mask to the black-on-yellow bat emblem on his chest. "I realize your interest in the situation, but at the moment I'm unable—"

"We both have an interest in this situation," Batman continued, his still-calm voice somehow cutting Winter off midsentence. "We both want to know about the murder."

"Yes," Winter countered as quickly as he could manage, "but with my schedule—"

"Winter." Batman's cape rustled as he took a step into the room. Winter found himself staring at the ashtray on the corner of his desk. "There's every possibility that I might be able to shed some light on the murder, to find some connection between this man and what happened in my past." A black-clad fist hit the desk, sending the ashtray off the edge. It made no sound when it hit the carpet. "But we have to do it *now*."

"Yes." Winter could no longer smile, but he forced himself to look up at the mask. He had to get rid of this man. He couldn't do anything with Batman here.

Winter cleared his throat. "Well, we'll—uh—have to do something about this, won't we?"

He picked up the phone as it started to ring.

"Samson," he answered. It was the only name he ever used.

"We lost one of our boys," his boss's voice drawled on the other end of the line. "It's so upsetting when you break up a set."

There was silence on the other end of the line. Sometimes Samson wished his boss could come right out and say what he was thinking.

"You want another one?" Samson asked.

"I'm not calling for my health," the boss snapped.

"Same terms?" Samson asked quickly. He didn't like to rile the boss. The guy might be crazy, but he was very generous—generous enough for Samson to stick around.

"We may even be able to give you a raise," his boss purred. "We're going up in the world, Samson. We need to recruit somebody special this time around." He hesitated, like a kid in a candy store, Samson thought, thinking of the best way to spend his dollar bill.

"Somebody prominent. Somebody with money? Oh, no no no, we have more than enough money, don't we?" The boss chuckled. "Well, we do, for the moment." He paused and sighed. "Let's see. This time we need someone with political connections. But who to choose?"

The boss was silent for a moment. Samson was quiet, too. He'd heard how bad it could get if you interrupted the boss at the wrong time.

"Hmm," the boss said at last. "Commissioner Gordon is out of town so much these days. And the mayor, perish the thought! He'd be too stupid to know how to put on the cape. No, I think we have to aim our sights a little lower. I think a mayoral assistant would be just the thing. And what good practice it will be for when we do get around to snatching Gordon?"

The laugh on the other end of the line was cut off abruptly. There was a click and a dial tone. His boss had given his orders, and Samson would carry them out. One of the mayor's assistants shouldn't be hard—the mayor had a bunch of them. And after that, he got to do Gordon?

Samson was really looking forward to that.

2

The man in the darkened room hung up the phone.

A mayoral assistant—what an inspired choice! He had always wanted to get into politics. And it was such a nice step up in his plans. He had such thorough plans, for Gordon, for the mayor, for Batman, even for Samson.

This felt so good! It was the best plan he'd ever had— the best game he had ever played.

Before this was over, he'd have plans for everyone in Gotham City.

There were the usual flashing lights and yellow police lines, with a dozen bored-looking policemen holding back the crowds of curious citizens. But the crowds moved out of the way, the policemen stood taller—everything changed when Batman arrived.

He let Winter lead the way into the First Gotham Bank.

It was quite gratifying how quickly they had gotten here. Batman didn't like to use intimidation, but sometimes, when he ran into someone like this so-called mayoral assistant, results became more important than methods.

The bank had been closed for the day, and Batman only had to walk into the lobby to see why. The heavy steel door that normally covered the vault on the main floor was now resting at a forty-five-degree angle to the vault itself. It looked as if both the lock and the hinges had been blown away—each with a small, precise explosion. The robbers had been professionals.

The explosion. No, he couldn't get there fast enough.
Batman closed his eyes.
Jason! Don't go in there. Jason Jason Jason.
But Jason couldn't listen. Jason Todd was dead.

Batman opened his eyes and took a deep breath. The vision had only taken an instant; the same vision that haunted his dreams. Jason Todd—the boy who had become the second Robin—dead at the hands of The Joker. And there was nothing Batman could do about it. Nothing but go on.

Winter was a dozen paces in front of him. The mayor's assistant hadn't even noticed anything was wrong. Batman took a few long strides to catch up.

He had a job to do.

As the two men crossed the inlaid marble floor, Winter repeated essentially the same information Batman had read in the morning paper; that the criminals had been all over the place, cleaning out both vaults and the safe deposit boxes. Very neat, very efficient—so efficient, in fact, that Batman was sure the criminals had used inside information. They had to have been in contact with someone who had worked here before, or perhaps even worked here still.

"Before we go any further," Winter declared, "we'd better go over this with the bank officials. This should only take a minute. Their offices are over this way."

Winter turned and marched to the right. Batman let him go.

Batman imagined the mayor's assistant wanted him to follow. But Batman could meet bank officials anytime. He had spotted somebody else who could be a hundred times more helpful.

He walked quickly toward the skinny man in the loud sportcoat who was kneeling in the back corner of the room. Nobody got in his way. Nobody ever questioned Batman.

"Batman?" Lieutenant Carmichael grinned up from where he studied a ragged black hole in an ornate brass door, a hole that must have once held an old but solid lock. "This was an inside job." He chuckled. "But you already knew that, didn't you?"

Carmichael was a good cop, efficient, no-nonsense, close to twenty years on the force; the very opposite of somebody like Winter. It was too bad that the Carmichaels of the world never ran the show. But Gotham City today was all image, in the hands of media men like the mayor and all his cronies. It was a fact of modern life. Even Batman played into his image.

Batman nodded at the charred metal by Carmichael's face. "They came in through this door?"

The police detective straightened up with a groan. "It didn't take much." He pointed at a thick bolt—still intact—pulled back from the top of the door. "Somebody left the dead bolt open on the inside." He scratched at his thinning hair. "I don't figure it. With the size of the hole they blew in this door, these guys were professionals. Why not cut through the dead bolt too and divert suspicion from the bank employees? It's like they wanted all of us to know it was an inside job.''

Batman nodded. It fit with his theory. There was something that still bothered him.

''But why did they have to disable one lock and not the other?'' he asked. ''Why didn't the inside contact simply leave the door open?''

This time, Carmichael scratched at the half of his head that still had hair. ''Good question. I figure that whoever was on the inside wasn't that high up in the organization.'' He pointed at the ragged hole that once held the lock. ''Only the top three bank officers had this key.''

Interesting. ''Was Cranshaw one of the three?''

Carmichael's eyebrows rose in surprise. ''The dead guy? Yeah, he was. That crazy old coot. What could make a guy, a bank vice president no less, dress up in a Batman suit?'' Carmichael grinned. ''Uh, no offense, Batman.''

''None taken.'' It was Batman's turn to smile.

''*There* you are, Batman!'' Winter called from across the bank. ''We must have crossed communications somewhere. No matter. I've brought somebody along who might be able to help us.''

As Bruce Wayne, he would have groaned. He knew the very well-dressed, middle-aged man with Winter all too well, the sort of man who could take up a great deal of time and keep Batman from observing what had really happened the night before. Bruce Wayne had money invested in half a dozen of the large Gotham City banks, First Gotham included. He had to talk to bankers like the one so nervously approaching. Batman didn't have the luxury of that sort of time.

''George T. Gerbasi,'' the banker reintroduced himself. ''Senior vice president.

"I can't imagine how this sort of thing could have happened," Gerbasi began in that anxious way he had. He coughed, looking from Winter to Batman, then quickly back to Winter again. "Well, actually, I can imagine, all too well. Bank robbery is an unfortunate fact of life for financial institutions. Some of our smaller branches have been robbed by masked gunmen, hit-and-run sort of things, but I never thought our main branch—I mean, this building was constructed so that—"

"I understand," Batman replied, wanting to cut off the banker as soon as possible. "Why don't we take a look at the burglars' handiwork?"

"Well, yes," Gerbasi replied after a second, apparently unsettled by Batman's interruption. "You'll have to excuse me. This has all been a little disturbing. I suppose that what you suggest would be appropriate. I have so little experience—"

"If we find out how it was done, we can make sure it never happens again."

"Uh—most assuredly. Let me show you the place where we—uh—found Cranshaw."

Gerbasi led the two other men behind the teller's cages and through another brass door that led to a staircase going down.

"The employee entrance to the safe deposit boxes. Authorized personnel have much more privileged access to a place like this." Gerbasi paused to stare suspiciously at the wrought-iron staircase. "I suppose the criminals must have known that, too."

Batman asked the next question as gently as he could: "Have you considered that someone inside the bank might have been passing the criminals information?"

The vice president's face drained of whatever color had

remained. "You mean somebody in First Gotham's—one of our bank employees? Oh, dear. Well, I certainly realize that is a possibility, but I would hate to think—that is—the First Gotham likes to treat our employees like a family!"

Batman kept himself from smiling. "Every family has a skeleton in its closet, Mr. Gerbasi."

"Oh," the vice president replied as he smoothed non-existent wrinkles from his three-piece suit. "Oh, dear." He stepped quickly to the railing and pointed down. "If you look from here—uh—you can see it."

Batman stepped up next to Gerbasi.

There, three long stories down, outlined with chalk on the dark grey floor, was the place where Cranshaw had fallen and died.

"And I understand from the coroner he fell from up here?" Winter asked.

"Shall we go down and take a look?" Batman asked.

"Oh, I suppose we should," Gerbasi agreed without much enthusiasm.

"Tell me, Mr. Gerbasi," Batman asked as they began their descent. "Are any of your employees missing?"

"Missing?" Gerbasi paused for a minute, and the only sound was the pounding of Gerbasi's and Winter's leather shoes on the wrought-iron stairs. Batman's soft rubber boots made no sound.

Gerbasi frowned as he looked back up at Batman. "Not that I know of. I'd have to check with personnel."

"Wasn't there some employee who was here during the robbery?" Winter asked the vice president. "Somebody who got hit on the head and tied up?"

"Sweeny? Oh, poor Bill. We did our best to keep that out of the papers. Bill's been with this bank as long as I have. Poor fellow, he was pretty shaken by the whole thing. He should be grateful to be alive, that's what I say."

This was the first Batman had heard about Sweeny. *Kept out of the papers*. This was why he had to get to the scene of a crime as soon as possible; especially a crime like this. What else had he missed?

Gerbasi started to explain how the robbers had systematically ransacked the safe deposit boxes, but Batman was only half listening. He needed to have a talk with this Sweeny—if he could still find him.

The man in the dark stood up and shook himself. The plan didn't allow him time to gloat—not yet. He had to make sure Batman was ready for tonight's job. He laughed. Things were so much easier when you ran absolutely everything. Oh, he wished he could see Batman's face when he finally figured out his part in all of this.

But what was he thinking about? He could not only see Batman's face—he could make that face do whatever he wanted.

Oh, this was a beautiful plan.

3

Gordon had to admit it; he rather liked showing up unexpectedly. The element of surprise appealed to the crusader inside him—catch them when they're not looking and you'll learn the truth.

"Commissioner Gordon!" O'Neal gulped down his water and trotted back from the cooler to his office.

Gordon closed the door behind him and walked into the outer office. Ms. Davis looked up at the commissioner and smiled. She raised that one eyebrow in that way she had. She didn't have to say a word. Gordon knew exactly what she was thinking: *You see what I have to put up with when you're gone.*

Gordon had finished with the convention early. As was so often the case in that sort of meeting, Gordon had learned everything he could from the Kansas City conference halfway through the weekend. He had been scheduled to run a seminar earlier this morning. Once that obligation was out of the way, he took the first available flight back to Gotham. Gordon didn't like to be away from his city any longer than was necessary.

He pulled off his raincoat and asked the same question he always asked his secretary.

"So, Ms. Davis, is the city still standing?"

His secretary smiled more warmly than before and gave her usual answer. "Just barely."

Ms. Davis was being her usual honest self. Gordon sometimes wondered how a city the size of Gotham could continue functioning without collapsing under its own weight. He looked down the row of offices. The small one in the corner was dark. "I see that our mayoral assistant is out."

"Ah," Ms. Davis replied with a remarkably satisfied sigh. "Now there's a story I have to tell you about."

Gordon found himself simultaneously amused and annoyed as Ms. Davis related the story about how Winter had tried to put Batman in his place, and how the masked vigilante had turned the tables, sending both of them to the First Gotham Bank.

"They're out there now?"

She nodded. "At the bank."

"Get them on the phone, would you? I'll make sure Batman gets whatever he needs."

The commissioner was not pleased with Winter's attempt to exclude Batman. Gordon had always considered the mayor's assistant a thorn in his side, an annoyance, nothing more. This time, though, Winter had done something potentially dangerous. The last thing in the world the commissioner wanted to do was alienate Batman—especially now, with the strain Batman was under.

But Batman would pull through it. He always had before. Unfortunately, the police commissioner couldn't say the same thing for his town.

It was Gordon's firm conviction that without Batman there would no longer be a Gotham City.

The white-jacketed attendant's face lit up as the two of them walked into the room. And Winter knew by now that her smile wasn't for him.

"We need to see Cranshaw," Batman announced.

The attendant stood quickly. Winter automatically read her name badge: Wendy Goodis.

"Oh, certainly. We were expecting you hours ago." She pushed her short grey hair out of her eyes and took three steps toward the inner door. "This way, please." Almost as an afterthought, she smiled at Winter. "And this is?"

"Steven Winter," he answered with his own smile and outstretched hand. "Mayor's assistant."

She ignored his hand but nodded pleasantly enough. "Any friend of Batman is a friend of ours." She turned and opened the inner door. "We figure, the more we can show him, the more he keeps our business here from getting out of hand. Fewer autopsies, more coffee breaks, that's our motto, huh, Batman?"

The attendant led the way into the city morgue.

Winter was gaining more respect for Batman with every moment they spent together. Every place Batman went, people knew him, or knew of him. No matter where Batman wanted to go or whom he wanted to talk to at the

First Gotham Bank, he got it without red tape and long explanations. This man had the kind of presence that could make a politician die from envy. Maybe, Winter realized, he could learn something from this man in a mask.

The cold air hit him in the face as he passed through the doorway, the temperature a good thirty degrees below that in the outer office. This was the first time Winter had ever been inside a morgue. Almost everything was white: the tiles on the walls, the fluorescent lights overhead, the painted cement floor, the large steel drawers with names scrawled with magic marker on masking tape, names like "John Doe #33." There were four white gurneys scattered about the room, and each gurney held a long canvas bag, all white again except for those blue toes that peeked from the bags' open ends, each foot sporting a neatly lettered, white name tag.

"We're a little overcrowded today," Wendy said, waving at the body bags. "All the drawers are full. No room at the inn." She stepped over to one of the gurneys. "Cranshaw might have been a big-time banker, but for now all he gets is a slab."

"Sam!" she called to an elderly man who pecked at a typewriter in the far corner of the room. "Could you give me a hand here? I need to show off one of our guests."

"Hey, Batman!" The old fellow rose from his seat and walked, stiffly but quickly, over to the others. As he approached, Winter noticed how pale his skin was, as if, with age, he was fading to the color of the morgue around him. "You got here just in time. They're gonna cut the banker up in another half an hour." He nodded at Winter, then winked conspiratorially. "Batman likes to see 'em before the autopsy. Lots of times, they stuff things back in the wrong way when they sew 'em up." He chuckled. "Sure can be a mess."

Sam hoisted the body as Wendy removed the bag, quickly, efficiently, without emotion. They must have done this job a thousand times.

Winter realized he'd never seen a cold, dead body before. The corpse that had been Cranshaw was naked, its plentiful flesh a sickly greyish blue. The man had been quite a bit overweight, and his fat rose in rolls about his midsection, creating little lines of shadow across the grey flesh in the places where it bunched together. The banker's eyes and mouth were open, as if he were surprised to find himself here.

It was the expression on his face that did it to Winter. The mayor's assistant felt the bile rise in his throat. He looked away and took a deep breath. He couldn't lose it now, not in front of Batman.

The phone rang, so loud in the silence of the morgue that it made Winter flinch. Sam quickly returned to his desk and picked up the receiver before it could complete its third ring.

"Morgue. Oh, sure, Commissioner. He's right here." He looked up at the group gathered around Cranshaw. "Batman?"

The masked man nodded. "I'm done here, anyway. Do you still have this man's—belongings?"

"You mean the Batman suit?" Wendy replied with another smile. "I've got it out in the office. The police want it for evidence."

Batman turned to Winter. "I'll meet you out there."

Another time, Winter might have objected to that sort of abrupt dismissal. Now, though, he was just glad to get away from the body. He walked back to the office. Wendy followed after him.

"Commissioner?" Batman said into the phone.

Wendy closed the door.

"You work for the mayor," she said, more a statement than a question.

"Well, yes," Winter began.

"Never see the mayor down in the morgue," she replied abruptly, turning away from Winter as if she had completely covered the subject. "Now, I've got that bat suit around here somewhere. It's a pretty pitiful-looking thing."

The door to the morgue opened and Batman stepped out. He looked straight at Winter.

"The commissioner wants to see you when you get back to the office."

"Ah, here it is!" she cried in triumph as she lifted a coffee mug from atop an opaque plastic bag. "You leave anything around here too long, it gets covered over." She picked up the bag, brushing off the droplets of spilled coffee. "Everything that was on the body, we put in here."

Batman opened the bag and pulled out the mask.

"Pretty pitiful, huh?" Wendy asked.

Winter decided he had to agree. The mask was badly cut and sewn—the stitching was already coming loose on one side, and one of the bat ears was twice the size of the other.

"The rest of the costume's just as bad," she assured Batman.

"I've got to see it for myself. You never know what you're going to find." Batman pulled the rest of the folded grey fabric free from the bag. Something yellow fell on the floor. Batman knelt to pick it up.

"A flower?" He held the yellow rose up with his gloved hand. The flower rustled when he stroked it with his other thumb. "A paper flower?"

The morgue attendant nodded, serious at last. "We found it tucked inside Cranshaw's mask."

Winter frowned at the small paper rose. He'd seen that kind of flower somewhere before.

He remembered avoiding that young man this morning on his way to work. He looked over at Batman.

"You see these fake flowers all the time, outside City Hall."

"Really?" Batman smiled coldly, a not-altogether pleasant sight. "Mr. Winter, I believe you can help me solve this case."

Samson knew a million ways to do a job.

Sometimes you went with your gut. Sometimes it was just luck. And sometimes, like now, it was like somebody was giving you a sign.

Samson had wandered casually down to City Hall, to do what the boss called "a little research." He needed to get a closer look at the mayor's assistants and their habits. But before he was halfway down the street, what should show up but the Batmobile?

Samson fought down the urge to cut and run. What could he be afraid of? There would be no way Batman could recognize him. After all, his record was clean. He'd never been convicted of a single thing in this part of the country.

It only took him a moment to be really glad he stayed.

For who should get out of the Batmobile's passenger seat but one of the mayor's assistants? Winter—that was his name. Samson recognized him from the photos the boss had sent over.

Samson had to keep from laughing. The boss would give him a bonus for this one. Not just a mayoral assistant, but Batman's personal mayoral assistant.

How could he possibly snatch anybody else?

4

Dick Grayson had thought that it couldn't get any worse. He realized now that he was wrong.

He looked at the paper in his hands. THE BATMAN MURDER, the headline read. A sensationalistic headline, nothing more than a sleazy way to sell newsprint.

The moment Dick read it, he felt like he'd been kicked in the stomach.

Batman wasn't dead, of course. The article talked about some middle-aged businessman who had gotten it into his head to dress up in a bat costume and had gotten killed for his fantasy.

But death was so close. It had only been a few weeks since Jason Todd—the second Robin—had been killed. And it was only with Jason's death that Dick Grayson, who had once been Robin himself, realized how much he had identified with the youngster. He had given one of his old Robin uniforms to Jason, had encouraged the kid, had thought it would be good for Batman to have a partner again. Without Dick Grayson's help, Jason Todd might never have become Robin.

Without Dick Grayson, Jason Todd might still be alive today.

No. There was no way he could have known Jason would die. There was no way he could blame himself. At least, that's what his psychiatrist said. But somehow, deep inside, the shame and blame were still there. Just as, somehow, he still blamed himself for the deaths of his parents.

He could see it now. His parents, swinging from trapeze to trapeze, high above the crowd, working without a net. He had just turned ten, and had been a regular part of the act for over a year, but he had been standing on the sidelines while his parents finished their specialty routine.

The crowd had screamed.

He had looked up and seen the broken rope, and his parents falling, forever falling toward the too solid ground and their deaths.

And he had just stood there, helpless.

Dick had blamed himself even then. He probably would have done nothing but blame himself, if Batman hadn't come along.

Batman had seemed perfect to the ten-year-old Dick Grayson. He was every bit as acrobatic as Dick's parents, and his mind was as sharp as his body was strong. But, perhaps most important of all, Bruce Wayne had become Batman because he had lost his parents, too. Bruce showed Dick what he could be, if he only tried.

Dick had moved into Wayne Manor, and to the outside world, they were a guardian and his ward, but they were more than that. They were Batman and Robin—they were a team.

It was only when he had gotten older that Dick realized there had been problems with his life as a crime fighter. Batman didn't think about trouble, he acted on it. But if Dick had learned one thing from his shrink, it was this: If you ignored your emotions, they came back to haunt you.

And Batman, right now, was haunted. He didn't like to talk about what went on inside him, probably tried to not even think about it, but Dick could tell Bruce was tearing himself apart over the death of Jason. In fact, Bruce Wayne hardly seemed to exist anymore. His life had been consumed by Batman, patrolling the city night and day, facing down ever-greater dangers, almost as if, in risking his life, he might somehow atone for the teenager's death. But it was more than that. Bruce wasn't thinking clearly anymore. He was making mistakes. If Batman kept pushing himself like this, he was going to die, just like Jason.

And now somebody else had killed a Batman. And Dick was sure that was going to push the real Batman even closer to killing himself.

Night had fallen in Gotham City, and Steve Winter was still riding with a costumed hero. Batman's sleek, black car, so startling in the middle of the day, seemed to blend in with the darkness, as if night was where it belonged. They drove quickly and silently through the urban streets. Other cars moved aside or slowed to a crawl as Batman passed, the other drivers awed by the Batmobile.

After their trip to the morgue, Batman had decided it was time to find Sweeny. The caped vigilante had contacted Gordon, and the commissioner had offered to send his men around to pick Sweeny up, but Batman thought he could get some more interesting results if he faced the watchman in person.

To Winter's surprise, Batman had asked him if he wanted to come along. Winter was even more surprised when he discovered he wanted to see this through, and he had said yes. Winter found he liked this detective stuff even better than politics.

"Someone from inside the bank was involved in that robbery," Batman explained as he drove. "And it couldn't have been Cranshaw—the robbers had to force open a door for which Cranshaw had a key. The next most likely suspect is the only man who was in the bank at the time of the robbery—the night watchman."

"So you're going to try and get him to confess?"

Batman stopped his car in a no-parking zone.

"If he's still here. Actually, I expect him to be long gone by now, either with the other robbers or on his own. But if I take a look around Sweeny's apartment, I might get some clue to his current whereabouts."

Batman flipped a switch to pop open the gullwing doors.

"Coming?" he asked. "It wouldn't hurt to have some-body official along."

So that's what he was, Winter thought. Somebody of-ficial. He nodded and got out of the car.

Sweeny lived on the second floor of an old apartment building. The lock was broken on the downstairs door. They walked in without ringing the bell. Batman didn't want to give Sweeny any more warning than he had to.

Sweeny's apartment was directly across from the top of the stairs. The force of Batman's knock pushed the door in a couple of inches. Batman pointed silently down by the doorknob. Winter saw scratched wood and twisted metal. The lock had been forced open.

Batman put a finger to his lips to tell Winter to keep quiet, then gently, but firmly, pushed the mayor's assistant beyond the side of the door.

Batman gave the door a stiff push with his boot. It didn't budge. He backed up and gave the door a solid kick. The contact sounded like a gunshot in the quiet hall. The door still didn't move. Batman stepped quickly to the side of the door, waiting, Winter guessed, for real gunshots from the inside of the apartment.

There was no response—no gunshots, or voices, or sounds of movement. If there was anyone inside, they were very quiet.

"Well, we've announced our presence," Batman said softly. "We'll have to force our way in. There's something wedged against the door. Give me a hand."

Batman put one of his shoulders against the door. Winter did the same.

"Now," Batman said. They pushed together. The door gave another inch.

"Again." Winter threw all his weight into it, grunting with the effort.

Something thumped heavily on the other side. The door gave half a foot.

Batman was inside the room before Winter could ask him what to do next. Winter followed, and saw what had been holding the door.

A body in a night watchman's uniform lay on the bare floor where it had fallen. It had to be Sweeny. His eyes were as wide open as Cranshaw's had been, but his open mouth was stuffed with crumpled green paper. Winter saw

some more of the paper on the floor and realized the crumpled rectangles were fifty- and hundred-dollar bills.
Sweeny appeared to have literally choked on money.

"He probably tried to make it to the front door," Batman
said as he surveyed the room, "and died against it."

Winter sighed. Batman could probably tell all sorts of
things by looking around the room. All Winter could see
was a dead man.

"He won't be answering any questions," Winter replied.

The other man shook his head grimly. "Oh, no. He
already has answered the only question I had." Batman
pointed at the dead man's hand. "This whole thing was
meant for me."

Winter looked where Batman pointed, and saw that
Sweeny clutched a paper rose.

Big Mike wouldn't mess up this time.

The boss had sent for Big Mike to tell him about their
next job. The other guys said you didn't work for the boss
anymore once you messed up, but they had to be telling
fibs. The boss was all smiles.

The boss used to let Big Mike go out and get another
guy to be Batman. You're not the brightest guy, the boss
would say, but you sure are strong. Sometimes people
would break when Big Mike held them. Women broke
real easy. But the boss had saved him from the cops. He
hadn't meant to kill either one of those women. Or those
other women, before they sent him to the home.

Big Mike would always be grateful to the boss for saving
him. That's why he was glad to go out and find a new
Batman.

But Big Mike messed up the last time he went to find

Batman. How was he to know the guy had heart trouble? Why would Batman have heart trouble, anyway? That didn't even make sense to Big Mike.

But the boss was going to give him another chance. He was all smiles, even patted Big Mike on the back.

"Big Mike," the boss had said, "I have a little job for somebody with your talents." Big Mike liked it when the boss talked about his talents. "We've got a little break-in planned. There's money to be made!"

There's money, and Big Mike was going to handle it! The boss wasn't sore at him at all. Maybe, if Big Mike did a good job, the boss would forget all about Samson and give Mike his old job back.

"And, Big Mike?" the boss had added. "Whatever you do, wait for Batman to show up before you break in. After all, what's a robbery without Batman?"

5

Somebody was playing with Batman.

You didn't fight crime without making enemies. And some of those enemies thought they had a score to settle. There were so many different criminals in Batman's past, so many different scores. Who would put somebody in a Batman suit, only to kill him off?

Perhaps it had something to do with doubles. That sounded like the criminal pattern of Harvey Dent, the disfigured district attorney who became Two Face. Two Face's criminal methods involved doing everything in pairs. But why would even Two Face want to create a second Batman?

And then to kill him. *Jason. The explosion. Batman running. Too late, always too late. He saw the broken body of the boy who should never have become Robin. No!*

Death was too close to Batman. He wouldn't dwell on the death of Jason Todd. He couldn't bring Jason back. It served no purpose. He had to get on with his life.

He forced his mind back to the evidence, and what he had learned from the examination of the two bodies. Why had there been flowers? Seeing two of the artificial roses, Batman knew he had been meant to find them. They were more than clues. They were signs of some sort; warnings perhaps, or taunts.

He'd take apart one of these flowers in his lab and let the police examine the other. Between them, they'd find where they came from: from their distribution network back to their factory of origin, no matter where in the world they came from. He would discover every fact these paper roses held.

He wasn't sure, though, how he could determine the most important part—exactly what the flowers were supposed to signify. The only ones who could tell him that were the people who left the flowers in the first place; people who also left dead bodies. Murdered men and flowers that were never alive—a strange set of souvenirs.

Batman just hoped he could find out what they meant before he was presented with any more.

Gordon had the answer.

The commissioner nodded without surprise as Batman related what he had learned about the flowers from Winter. "The Church of Perpetual Happiness. We've been investigating them for some time. Come on into the conference room." He turned to look at his bookcase. "I can show you—I've got the videotape right here."

He pulled a tape from a row of a couple dozen, then led Batman into the room adjoining his office. He slid the tape into the VCR and turned on the monitor. He waved for Batman to take a seat, then grabbed a chair himself.

A picture formed as the monitor warmed, first static, then lines that resolved into a young man in his late teens or early twenties, holding one of those yellow roses.

"Hey, mister, buy a flower?"

The commissioner picked up a remote control from the conference table and pressed the pause button. "We trained a hidden camera on them for four hours," Gordon explained, "right here, in front of City Hall. After that, we didn't bother."

Didn't bother? Batman looked over at the commissioner.

"We edited the four hours down to about twelve minutes," Gordon went on, anticipating Batman's question. "You'll see why. It takes no time at all to figure out exactly what's going on." He punched the remote again.

"A flower?" asked another man, his back to the camera. "Is the money for charity?"

The young man nodded. "For hunger relief in Afghanistan," he said.

His face was replaced by that of a dark-haired young woman who nodded, too. "Shelter for the homeless," she said.

Another young male face, with an oriental cast to his features, spoke next from behind his flower: "To ship medical supplies to the tornado-ravaged south."

An even younger-looking, blond woman followed: "To help send the less fortunate through college."

"The flowers cost twelve cents apiece," Gordon interrupted the never-ending flow of sincere explanations. "They get two dollars for them, if not more."

"Oh, I'm sorry, sir," the pretty blond girl said innocently. "We don't give change."

"None of them are telling the truth," Gordon explained as he again froze the video image. "And all of them believe they're telling lies to promote some kind of 'greater good.' That's the kind of mind-set this sort of organization promotes in its members. As far as we can figure, all the money actually goes back into the church. After that, we have no idea what happens to the funds."

"Can't you close them down?" Batman asked.

"For what? Taking a dollar here and there by misrepresentation? At most, we could stick these kids—none of whom have criminal records—with a charge of petty larceny. What do we end up with—fifty-dollar fines? These kids can make more than that in a quarter of an hour. With our overcrowded courts, the D.A. decided it wasn't worth the trouble, at least at this level. Now"— Gordon's eyebrows went up as he paused—"if we could get at those higher up in this so-called church, that would be a different story."

The so-called church. Batman was aware of these supposedly "cult" organizations, but he had never had the time to investigate them directly.

"Do you think this church is behind these deaths?" he asked Gordon.

"Because of the flowers?" The commissioner grunted. "Why would they leave such an obvious calling card? No, it's far more likely that the flowers are being left by somebody who has a grudge against the church. An ex-member, a parent of one of the converts, perhaps somebody who's lost a lot of money to the organization, someone like that."

Batman wasn't so sure about Gordon's conclusions. "But who's to say what goes on inside these organizations? It's obvious from the bit of tape you've shown me that they operate in flagrant disregard for the law. They're using one of the basics our system is based on—freedom of religion—to hide their illegal activities. If you're already successful hiding fraud, perhaps money laundering, even graft, what's to stop you from hiding murder?''

Gordon considered this. ''Let me show you the next part of the tape,'' he said after a moment.

Music blasted from the monitor's stereo speakers. And what music. It was high, ethereal, almost classical in form, some sort of interplay of strings and horns that had to come from a synthesizer, played like Mozart on speed. Surprisingly, the final effect was fairly pleasing, sounding a bit like the laughter of angels.

The music flew into an even higher key, then faded, as if it had vanished onto some astral plane. The video screen was filled with a handsome, smiling, middle-aged man's face.

''Happiness is the key,'' he said.

''Good afternoon, joy seekers.'' An announcer's voice spoke from off-screen: ''Here are some words of truth from the Reverend Joey Droll.''

A crowd, also unseen, applauded and cheered wildly. The reverend, apparently, was talking to an audience of his followers. He waited politely for the adulation to subside. He nodded once it was silent, and, still smiling, began to speak:

''Could your life be more than it is today? Do you feel, somehow, that you are missing something? Maybe you never finished high school, are stuck in a dead-end job, and never seem able to get ahead. Or perhaps you graduated from that good school, and got that good job, and try to buy the good things in life. But you find once you buy that new car that it never goes fast enough. The new house has a leaky roof. And your husband, or your wife, why don't they treat you like they did before you were married? Why don't your kids treat you with respect? Why can't your parents understand that you're old enough to make your own decisions? If only you'd get those few things straight, you could be truly happy, couldn't you?''

The Reverend Joey Droll paused to smile even more benignly than before as he surveyed the audience.

"But is any one of us, you may ask, any one of us rich or poor, ever truly happy? Well, perhaps you weren't before you had the good fortune to turn on this program. But now that you have discovered the Church of Perpetual Happiness, that's all about to change.''

"Tell the truth, Reverend!'' someone yelled from the audience.

"Share the joy! Share the joy!'' a couple of female voices began to chant.

Droll nodded his head magnanimously. "Real happiness, pure joy, the end to all your troubles; that's the very thing I'm here to provide.''

Three bright yellow lines were superimposed over the lower third of the screen:

CALL NOW
1-600-555-1600
YOUR KEY TO HAPPINESS

Gordon hit the freeze button again.

"The Reverend Droll showed up in Gotham City about six months ago. His half-hour show began to appear at odd hours on UHF and cable outlets. Within a month, he'd bought an old elementary school and converted it into the church's headquarters. The kids showed up on the streets about that time, hawking the flowers. We believe, incidentally, that the street hawkers are only one small part of Droll's organization. As Droll's money situation improved, his show went to better and better outlets, at better and better times. And he kept on buying Gotham real estate.''

The commissioner looked back at the smiling, frozen image in the screen, then put down the remote control. ''The rest of the tape shows the highlights of Droll's show—happiness testimonials from the audience, repeated instructions on where you can send your happiness donation and receive the reverend's blessing—''

''I get the idea,'' Batman replied.

''We tried to plant a rookie in the organization a little while ago. He reported back to us once—the day after he went into the church. That was almost three weeks ago. We haven't heard from him, or seen him, since. We even managed to trump up a building inspection and searched the church headquarters. It was like he vanished from the face of Gotham City.''

''Why haven't you told me about this before?''

''I would have, if I thought there was some way for Batman to help.'' Gordon stood up and turned off the monitor.

Batman considered what he had seen. The commissioner was right. There were no cops and robbers here. This looked like a whole new level of crime.

He stared down at his gloves for a moment. ''There must be some way we can get inside their organization.''

''How?'' Gordon asked. ''We can't very well go in and ask. And I don't dare risk sending in somebody else undercover.''

Batman searched his mind for some ploy they had used

in the past to get inside someplace that was supposed to be impenetrable. He could arrange for Bruce Wayne to give the church a bequest. He dismissed the thought immediately. He wouldn't want to give the scam any publicity.

"I could join the church myself," he said.

Gordon dismissed the suggestion with the wave of his hand. "In some sort of disguise, I assume? You're too old. They'd take all your money and leave you outside the organization. The church takes their real recruits from the young and impressionable. They're easier to train, easier to indoctrinate with the church's true mission."

Gordon sighed and slumped in a chair. "These cults are everywhere in Gotham—everywhere in the country, I suppose."

Gordon's statement didn't surprise Batman in the least.

"Maybe I could get somebody with a couple more years of experience to volunteer, somebody that we could keep better tabs on. In good conscience, though, I don't know if I can expose anybody to that kind of manipulation without the proper training."

The proper training? Batman thought. It might be almost impossible to find the right combination of youth and mental toughness. Batman knew of only one very special person who might fit that assignment, and that person very likely would never talk to Batman again.

"Do we have to wait here all night?"

Big Mike shook his head. "Couple more minutes. Then we go in and steal the paintings. It's simple."

"Yeah," the other guy said. "It would have to be."

The other three gang members laughed.

"What do you mean by that?" their leader demanded. "Are you making fun of Big Mike? The boss put me in charge—the boss knows what he's doing!"

"The boss is crazy," the other guy shot back.

There was a noise up above them, somewhere on the roof of the museum.

Big Mike made an exaggerated shushing sound. "Batman's here. We can do it now."

The other crooks gathered up their gear. Big Mike wasn't going to let the others get off that easily. He was still angry.

He glared at the other members of his gang. "Because of what you said," he whispered hoarsely, "Big Mike's not going to let you have any fun. Because of what you said, you don't get to kill Batman." He jerked his thumb toward his chest. "Big Mike kills Batman!"

He smiled. That was telling them. Big Mike felt better already.

6

"I can't." Dick Grayson's chest felt so tight, he could barely say the words. Why couldn't he talk to this man? Why did he have to make up excuses? "I'm too busy with the Titans."

"I see," the voice on the other end of the line said without emotion. "Well, I'll have to make some other plan." There was a click and a dial tone.

Dick hung up the phone. He wanted to slam it back into the receiver.

Dick Grayson had been expecting this sort of call ever since he had read about the man murdered in the Batman costume. Why, then, was it so difficult to talk to Bruce? And why did he want to slug Batman in the jaw?

He supposed this all went back years, to a time when he thought everything was perfect—when his world was centered around Batman and Robin, keeping Gotham City safe from crime. But Batman broke up their team—coldly and abruptly—when Dick almost lost his life during a case. And part of Dick, at least, had accepted the break-up, even looked forward to getting out on his own. After all, what seemed perfect at fourteen could be holding him back by the time he finished high school. There came a time when Dick Grayson had to grow up.

So he joined the Titans, first as Robin, but then forging a new identity as Nightwing, starting what he hoped would be a whole new life as a part of the group. But his past was still a part of him. Even though he was a world away from Wayne Manor, he still compared himself to his mentor. Was this the way Batman would have handled it? Batman would have seen through that ruse right away. Couldn't Batman have solved this faster? Somehow, Nightwing always came up short.

This, Dick realized, was what was making him furious. Perfect. That's how he had always thought of Batman. That was the real reason Dick had become Nightwing, to try to be Batman all over again.

But Jason's death had changed all that.

Something had happened to Batman when his second Robin had been murdered. Batman had always solved crimes by balancing an analytical mind against a need for action. But Batman seemed to have less time now for analysis. In these last weeks, physical force had dominated over thought, and Dick watched Batman lash out blindly, as if violence could keep away the pain.

The pain—that was the real difference. Before this, Dick hadn't even known Batman was capable of feeling pain. Oh, he had seen Bruce go through physical pain. They had both gotten their share of bruises over the years. But emotional pain? Somehow he had thought Batman was beyond that. Dick guessed that his biggest shock in all of this was to find out that Batman was human. And not just human, but just as messed up as all the other humans.

Dick had tried to talk to Batman about this before. He had asked him why Bruce hadn't told him about Robin's death, why he had to find out about it somewhere else.

He had gone to meet his mentor in the Batcave. It had been strange for Dick, going to a place that used to mean so much to him. But the Batcave was also one of those things Dick had consciously left behind when he had moved on to become Nightwing. It felt awkward to be back there again.

Batman hadn't been exactly glad to see him, either. "I didn't expect to see *you* again" was his only greeting.

But Dick hadn't wanted an argument. "I heard about Jason," he said instead. "I'm really sorry, Bruce."

"You weren't at the funeral" was the blunt reply. "People asked about you."

Dick had found himself getting frustrated. There were reasons he couldn't come to the funeral. He had been busy as Nightwing, something he didn't think Batman even wanted to hear. "Come on, Bruce, talk! Don't turn your back on me. I'm here—now."

But Batman still wouldn't look at him. "You were lucky. When you didn't listen to me, your injuries weren't fatal. Of course, by the time I *properly* trained you—"

Dick remembered how angry he felt at the other man's coldness. "Bruce, come on. Lay off. I'm not here to fight you—"

"Then don't."

Something snapped in Dick, the same sort of thing that made him leave Wayne Manor. "Are you blaming me? I left, so Jason replaced me, and because I left he died?"

He laughed coldly. "No way, pal. Jason wasn't me." That's when he said the things he shouldn't have, the words coming from his emotions, not his head. "I was a trained acrobat. I could think quickly in perilous situations. But Jason? Why did you let him become Robin before he was ready?"

Batman had spun to face him at last. "Don't you dare blame me for Jason's death! Don't you dare!"

Bruce had ended up taking a swing at him, as if Dick's question had been some sort of physical assault, then gone on to shout about why he ever thought he needed a partner. At the end there, Batman wasn't making sense, just letting the rage come out.

It was the first time Dick had ever seen the other man so illogical, so unreasonable—

So human.

When it came to Jason Todd, Batman couldn't think about his troubles or confront his emotions. For the first time, Dick realized that Bruce might be afraid of thinking, that maybe Bruce blamed himself for the deaths of Dr. and Mrs. Wayne just as Dick felt guilty for what happened to his own parents. But Dick, at least, had been seeing a therapist for his problems. He was dealing with his grief. Batman, though, had no place for his problems to go. He was filled with a rage that someplace, some time, would have to explode; the sort of rage that could destroy someone—even somebody like Batman.

What would happen if Batman couldn't take it anymore? Could Gotham City survive?

Big Mike would make the boss proud. The keys fit the locks, the alarms were just where they were supposed to be, the night watchman was tied and gagged before he could do a thing.

Mike sent the boys off to cut the right paintings from their frames, and steal the best stuff out of the cases. Most of it seemed like so much junk to Mike—who wanted old vases and bowls anyway? But the boss said he had buyers. And money always made the boss happy. So Big Mike would get the boss money.

Everything else was ready. Now Big Mike had to take care of the new Batman. The last guy fell over the railing to smash on the floor down below. Well, he was dead, that was what the boss wanted, but Big Mike wasn't happy. He was only happy when he could really squeeze.

So this time he waited in the dark coatroom, waited for Batman to walk in the door so he could go out and greet him with open arms.

"Hey!" one of the boys yelled from inside the museum. "Look out!"

"It's the Batman guy!" another one added. Then he screamed.

Big Mike frowned. The new Batman had come in another way? It wasn't supposed to be like this. Big Mike let out a long breath. He couldn't wait for Batman anymore. He'd have to go out and find him.

He stepped out of the dark and walked down the hall toward the big room with all the paintings. The bright lights that they left on in the museum threw huge shadows against the white walls. It made him feel like a giant.

"Don't hide from Big Mike, Batman!" he yelled ahead. "Big Mike wants to be your friend!"

He'd give Batman that last big hug.

Big Mike loved the sound of breaking bones.

* * *

The alarm had sounded halfway through dinner.

Bruce hurried into the cave to check his bank of computers. As he had suspected, somebody had tripped one of what he liked to think of as his "insurance alarms." After the job at the First Gotham Bank, he had taken a couple dozen of his own miniature sensing devices and placed them around Gotham City, in banks, museums, mansions—anyplace that would seem to have a particularly sophisticated security system, like the First Gotham Bank. That way, if someone disabled any of the other security systems, they would automatically trip one of Batman's personal alarms.

And so they had. According to the flashing light, somebody had broken into the Gotham Institute of Art.

He was in uniform and in the Batmobile in less than a minute. He decided he'd notify the police when he reached the museum.

This time, he wanted a few minutes alone with these particular criminals.

7

Big Mike clumped heavily through the museum. He liked the way his boot steps echoed in this big building. The noise made him sound even larger than he really was.

"Oh, Batman!" he called in his happy singsong. "Where are you, Batman?"

Big Mike was really enjoying himself. He wished he could kill a Batman every day of his life.

He stepped into the big room with all the paintings. The bright lights showed two of his gang flat on the floor. They were both out cold. Big Mike smiled. He liked a challenge. This Batman was going to be even more fun than the one at the bank.

He heard something rustle at the far end of the room, saw movement in the shadows where the emergency lights didn't reach.

"Now, now, Batman." He walked quickly toward the shadows. "It's not nice to hide from Big Mike."

Somebody turned out the lights. It was very dark. The only light came from a row of windows close to the ceiling.

"You want to play games? Big Mike likes to play games." He wasn't feeling as good about this as he was before. It would be harder to find this guy without any lights. And didn't the boss say something about all the lights were run from a switchboard in the front of the museum? Yeah, that's right, Big Mike had seen the big board, right next to the coatroom.

But how had this Batman guy turned out the lights if they were way back there?

Big Mike wasn't happy. Why couldn't he grab something? Why couldn't he crush something?

"Looking for me?"

Big Mike ducked as something swung over his head. Good thing Big Mike was so fast. His eyes were getting used to the dark. He saw a shape overhead. The shape reached for him.

Big Mike rolled. He jumped up to a crouch and ran even farther away.

There was a hand on his shoulder. The hand wore a glove.

"I heard you calling my name," another voice said softly.

"Batman?" Big Mike whispered. He had just gotten away from him on the other side of the room. How could this guy move so fast? Unless—

There were two of them in here! Cripes!

That meant one of these batmen was the real thing!

*   *   *

Dick Grayson looked out into the darkness.

Jason Todd was dead, and no amount of anger would bring him back. Batman wasn't ready to face up to it. If somebody was going to make peace, it would have to be Dick.

His whole life had changed when he learned the second Robin had died. He had moved out from his girlfriend's apartment, told his friends and teammates he needed some time alone. He had to think why his life had led him here, and what he needed to do next.

Robin was dead.

Sure, it had been a second Robin. But, before that, Dick had been Robin. It could have been him. Maybe that's all that it was. Maybe he still thought, deep down inside, that there might have been some way he could have saved Jason.

Dick was confused and angry, and—now that he'd cooled down a little—he realized he was just as much to blame as Bruce for the fights they had had. Nobody was perfect here. Everybody made mistakes.

Maybe he had made a brand-new mistake by not talking to Batman on the phone. Dick needed to find a way to get through to Bruce, to get him to think as well as act. To do that, maybe Dick needed to get back into the action, too. Maybe he needed to get down and dirty in the streets again.

Yeah. It felt right. Dick would call Batman back and tell him he'd help in the investigation of this so-called church.

Gordon was startled when someone knocked on his office door. It was almost midnight, and he had stayed late to catch up on the work he had missed by going to the conference. He hadn't thought there was anyone else in this part of the building.

He quietly opened the desk drawer that held his .38.

"Come in," he called.

The door opened and Steven Winter stepped inside.

Gordon knew there was something wrong. For the first time since Winter had been assigned to this office, the mayor's assistant wasn't smiling.

"Commissioner?" he asked. "We need to talk." He walked over to the far side of Gordon's desk. "As you know, I've been keeping up with this Batman murder case and the theoretical involvement of the Church of Perpetual Happiness."

The mayor's assistant placed a folded piece of paper on his desk.

"See what I got," Winter said.

Gordon opened the creased paper—a simple 8 ½-by-11 sheet, folded as if it had been stuffed into a regular number ten envelope. A business letter.

"Dear Mr. Winter," the letter read. "We at the Church of Perpetual Happiness have long admired your work for the community of Gotham City, and would like to extend an invitation to a special celebration in your honor—"

Gordon frowned. Did this mean something? He looked up at Winter.

"Coincidence?" he asked.

Winter shrugged and tried to smile. "Probably. It's the sort of thing I'd normally just throw in the trash—a fringe organization looking for publicity, you know. But seeing as how you want to get inside the church, I thought it might be useful—"

"Certainly," Gordon replied as he scanned the rest of the letter. There didn't seem to be anything sinister here. Indeed, there didn't even seem to be anything out of the ordinary. "I assume, of course, that you will need a police escort to this event."

"At the very least," Winter replied. "I'd also like to invite Batman."

Gordon handed the paper back to the mayor's assistant. "Mr. Winter. I think that can be arranged."

Winter stuck the letter into his inside jacket pocket. "I'm looking forward to it." He turned and left the room.

Gordon spent a long moment looking at the door the mayor's assistant had so recently closed. Steven Winter was beginning to surprise him.

Batman had given the room a quick scan with his infrared lenses. There were two bodies on the floor—unconscious, but breathing. He stood over a third man who squatted on the floor. The man below him was short but solidly built, almost all muscle. From the way the man shifted, Batman was expecting him to spring. There was somebody else here, too, hiding behind the sculpture at the far side of the room.

"No Batman's gonna take me!" the man near his feet screamed. Batman backed off just enough to let the muscle-bound fellow jump to his feet, then connected a solid punch to the man's jaw. Muscle-bound or not, the man collapsed on the floor.

"You." The other man stepped out of hiding. "Who are you?"

"I'm Bat—" he began, but his voice stopped as he saw the other man's costume. The other man was wearing a cape and a cowl, not unlike Batman's own.

"I require an answer," the other man spoke harshly as he stepped forward. "I warn you. I'm Batman."

The real Batman almost smiled. Another imposter? Maybe this whole thing would fall into place.

The muscle-bound hood groaned as the false Batman stepped over him.

In the meantime, though, Batman had to consider what to do with this imposter.

"What?" the false Batman demanded as he came closer. "What is the meaning of your costume?"

The hood started to struggle to his feet. Batman decided this all might be amusing, if it wasn't so dangerous. How could he explain things to this man pretending to be him?

"Look," he began. "You have to understand something—"

"You haven't answered my question!" The new Batman grabbed the real costumed hero's arms. "Who are you? There can only be one Batman!"

The hood had regained his feet.

"Look out!" Batman yelled as he pushed the imposter out of the way.

But the imposter kept his grip on Batman's left arm, twisting it painfully behind the hero's back.

"You're not going anywhere," the imposter murmured, "until I'm finished with you."

"I don't care which one of you is real," the hood said from half a dozen feet away. He pulled a gun from inside his jacket. "I'm going to blow you both away."

"Fool!" Batman yelled at the other man. The pain in his arm increased as he tried to shift his weight. "Let me move before we get shot!"

If anything, the other man's grip tightened.

"Nobody calls Batman a fool."

The real Batman looked down the barrel of a Magnum.

"Hey," the hood said cheerfully. "Maybe Big Mike can kill two batmen with one bullet! The boss would like that a lot."

He squeezed the trigger.

8

Batman threw his weight forward, twisting to his left to relieve the pressure on his arm.

"Wha—" the false Batman said as the gun went off.

Batman felt fire in his shoulder. Startled, the false Batman had let go of his arm. Batman tucked his chin into his neck and used his forward momentum to somersault straight into the startled Big Mike.

Mike grunted as his hands flew up. The gun went off a second time, shattering glass in the skylight far overhead.

"You're hurt!" the false Batman screamed. "Nobody hurts anybody when Batman is around!"

The real Batman used his good arm to push himself up from the floor. He needed to get the gun away from Big Mike.

"Out of the way!" the false Batman yelled behind him. "You're obstructing justice!"

Something struck Batman at the base of the skull. He staggered forward. Without the padding under his cowl, the blow would have knocked him cold.

The false Batman pushed him out of the way as he rushed Big Mike.

Batman shook his head, trying to clear it. He had to get in there before someone got hurt.

"You!" the imposter yelled. "You're going to learn that nobody crosses Batman!"

There was another gunshot.

Batman stood as the false Batman fell onto Big Mike.

Big Mike pushed the false Batman away. Batman could tell the other man was dead.

"Big Mike's shot too many bullets." The hood leveled the gun at Batman. "The boss isn't happy when Big Mike uses too many bullets. Waste not, want not, the boss always tells Big Mike."

Big Mike had already used one bullet too many on Batman. Batman's boot lashed out, the toe catching Big Mike's wrist.

The hood yelled as his Magnum went flying. The gun clanged against a metal sculpture before falling to the floor.

Big Mike roared and slammed Batman in his wounded shoulder. Batman staggered back, his breath gone with the searing pain. But he was still standing.

The hood looked wildly around the room. "Big Mike needs his gun."

Batman walked forward. "Big Mike needs a jail cell."

His comment seemed to hit some sort of nerve. "Big Mike's not going back to jail! Big Mike's never going back to jail!" The crook slammed against Batman's wounded shoulder again.

Damn. He staggered back a step, then shook his head

clear. The wound didn't seem that bad. He was still standing. But his shoulder was covered with blood, and his vision seemed to fog with that last blow. He wasn't sure how long he could keep up with Big Mike. He had to take him out now.

He stepped out of the way of the thug's next blow as he covered his wounded shoulder with his cape. The big man stared openmouthed as Batman stepped forward. He reached down to his utility belt.

"You're coming with me, Big Mike."

He popped open a small compartment and palmed a small electronic device.

"No! Big Mike only goes where he wants to go!"

Even in the dim glow from the skylight, Batman could see the look of terror on the criminal's face. He would get the terror to work for him.

Big Mike seemed frozen where he stood. Batman walked forward until he was within arm's reach of the crook. "What chance have you got against Batman if you can't find your gun?"

"Nobody takes Big Mike!" The crook threw another punch for Batman's wounded shoulder. Batman twisted away, throwing his cape around Big Mike's arm.

"No!" Big Mike shrieked. "Not taking me! Not taking me!" He jerked away wildly, then ran, stumbling, from the room.

Batman took a deep breath. In the moment he had had the frantic crook trapped, he had managed to snag the device in the lining of Big Mike's jacket. Now all he had to do was give the crook a little time, and he could reel him in, and maybe a few other fish besides.

He could hear sirens outside.

Batman went to turn on the lights.

* * *

Gordon walked quickly into the museum. He had left his office as soon as he had heard the police call.

Batman was waiting for him, along with half a dozen of Gordon's men.

His men had already captured two of the men who had broken in—Gordon had seen them in one of the squad cars outside. Both of them were small-time hoods with long records; not the kind of crooks you'd associate with this kind of sophisticated job. He stepped past the police lines, into the museum, and saw that the paramedics were fitting a large white bandage on Batman's upper arm. And on the far side of the room, he saw they had another dead man in a Batman costume.

The coroner had gotten there only a moment before, and was peeling back the hood to reveal the corpse's face.

Batman pulled himself free of the paramedic's attentions and walked over to join Gordon for the unveiling.

The costumed hero nodded. "Commissioner."

Gordon nodded back. They had investigated so many crimes together, there really wasn't any need to talk. "The arm?" he asked.

"Nothing serious" was the reply.

The coroner looked up as they approached. "Jim. Batman." He rubbed the palms of his hands together, knuckles against knuckles, then waved at the face he had just revealed. "Either of you know this guy?"

Gordon thought he looked familiar. "This guy worked for the museum, didn't he? He's had his picture in the paper a few times."

"George T. Herbert," Batman added. "Chief curator. Liked to spend his free time hiking and mountain climbing."

Gordon glanced appreciatively over at his old friend. Batman's memory for this sort of detail was astounding.

"He was in pretty good shape for a man in his middle fifties," the coroner rattled on. "You see the cause of death."

Gordon glanced at the hole a bullet had torn in the man's chest.

"It was a point-blank shot." The coroner paused again to clasp his hands. "Death would have been instantaneous."

Gordon squatted to get a better look at the body. Whatever was going on here, this guy seemed like a better choice to playact Batman than the last one. The costume was better sewn than the last one, too. In the dark it would look like a fair approximation of the real thing.

Gordon turned to Batman. "Can you tell me what happened here?"

Batman tersely recounted the fight and the robber who had gotten away.

Gordon looked up at a plainclothesman at his side. "Did they take anything?"

"Not so far as we can tell," the detective replied. "They cut a couple of pictures out of the frames, but we found them rolled up in a corner. Batman got here before they could get very far."

"I've got a question for you, Commissioner," Batman remarked. "Would you have any records on a criminal who calls himself Big Mike?"

"Big Mike? We can find out," Gordon replied. He looked back to the detective. It took him a second to remember his name. "Uh—Hennesey, go out to the car and feed the name into the computer as an aka."

The detective nodded and left the room.

"There's one more thing I should mention," Batman added quietly once they were alone. "I put an electronic tracing device on Big Mike, the man who got away. The man I let get away. With any luck, he'll lead us to the rest of the gang." He stepped back from the body. "So, if you'll excuse me, I have work to do."

Gordon stood up. He didn't want Batman doing this by himself. "You're wounded."

Batman looked down at the bandage the paramedics had put on his upper arm. "Only creased my shoulder. No serious damage."

But Gordon wouldn't let Batman go that easily. Batman had changed since Robin was killed. He was more abrupt in his actions, more brutal in his apprehension of criminals. There had been accidents and broken bones. Sometimes Gordon thought it was a miracle that none of the criminals had died.

It also seemed now that Batman had no time for the police, that he wanted to do everything himself. Gordon was willing to give his old friend some room, but they still had to follow procedure. It was understandable that Batman would feel a personal interest in this case, but robbery and murder were still jobs for the police. He couldn't let Batman's quest for justice interfere with Gotham City's law and order.

"We still need to work with you," Gordon insisted.

The caped hero seemed to stiffen. "Of course," Batman replied after a pause that meant that he, too, had made a decision. "I'll keep in touch with you from the Batmobile. Your men can follow me out. I'll radio to you if we get separated."

Gordon exhaled slowly as the hero marched from the room. He had always known that Batman had his demons, but now they seemed far too close to the surface. What would happen if Batman refused to work with the police? Would Gordon have to become an adversary to his old friend?

Batman climbed into the Batmobile and turned on the scanner. His miniature tracker was working perfectly. A small blue blip pulsed regularly in the top left-hand corner of the screen. That meant Big Mike had gone northwest, out to where Gotham City met the suburbs. Batman's fingers punched the right combination of buttons, and the Batmobile roared to life. It wouldn't do to let his prey get out of range.

George T. Herbert had been another acquaintance of Bruce Wayne's, another man who moved through the upper echelons of Gotham City society. There might be a pattern here. Batman would have to ask Commissioner Gordon if any other members of Gotham society had disappeared.

The strangest part of this was that Herbert had really believed he was Batman. The last time Bruce Wayne had seen the museum curator, he was regaling a cocktail party with mountain-climbing stories. Bruce had never known Herbert well, had actually considered the fellow a bit too self-important, but had never thought of the curator as someone who might be mentally ill. What would convince someone—especially someone with as strong a personality as Herbert—to take on another identity?

Batman hoped that Big Mike would show him the way to the answer. He pulled out of the museum's parking lot and headed for the highway. At this hour he could make up any time he'd spent talking to the commissioner. He and Big Mike should be meeting again soon.

He flipped a toggle switch on the dashboard to open a line to the police.

"Batman here. I'd like to speak to the commissioner."

"Certainly, sir." There was a moment of static, then a voice. "Batman? Gordon here."

"I believe our quarry is heading out Route 17. I'm moving to intercept him. I'll call you when I get close."

"Check," Gordon's voice replied. "We'll be right behind you."

Not too close, Batman thought. He wanted to do a little looking around before the police arrived.

A soft chime alerted him there was another call coming in. Only three people knew how to reach this mobile line and he was already talking to Gordon. Could it be Alfred?

"Batman out," he said to close off the first call, then flipped a switch to receive the incoming signal.

"Batman?" It was Dick's voice, of course.

"Nightwing," Batman replied. "Is this urgent?"

"It's urgent if you want the two of us to work together again." He could hear a hint of anger in the younger man's voice. Dick Grayson sighed. "Bruce, things have slowed down around here. I decided it wouldn't be a bad idea for me to get away. If you still want me to look into the church, I can give you a few days."

"Good," Batman replied. "I'm glad you changed your mind."

"Well," Dick admitted, "I guess I am, too."

"I'm following up on something now," Batman added. "Let's talk in the morning."

"I'm looking forward to it." Dick—Nightwing—broke the connection.

Batman realized he was looking forward to working together, too. As angry as he had been with his former partner, there was no one else Batman would trust more with this sort of job.

Perhaps, for a while at least, Batman wouldn't have to do everything himself.

9

Commissioner Gordon stopped his car at the entrance to the construction site. There hadn't been much construction here recently. The fence around the site was broken in places, and the large sign advertising the development was missing one of its supporting beams, so that it sagged seriously to the right.

RIVER POINT
LUXURY CONDOMINIUMS
Studio to Three Bedrooms, starting at $250,000.
Special Penthouses Available.
Opening—

There was a ragged edge after the last word, as if the final date had been torn away. Probably somebody's idea of a joke. Unless Gotham City's economy took a quick turnaround, these condominiums, and a dozen others on the outskirts of the city, would never open, ever. Beyond the fence, he could see a pair of dark, hulking shapes where a couple of the building units had been more or less completed, while beyond them were three more empty steel shells.

He waved the other three police cruisers on ahead, then climbed back into his car and followed them in through the open gate.

Gordon wondered absently which of the Gotham banks had had to take this project as a loss. With Gotham City's economy failing the way it was, there were a lot of these losses—ill-advised projects that had been begun in the boom years half a decade before. Now there didn't seem to be enough money to do anything with them—anything, perhaps, but act as temporary shelter for the homeless, and a perfect hiding place for crime.

He pulled his car up to join the other cruisers behind the Batmobile. Batman, of course, hadn't waited for them. Gordon got out of his car and joined his men.

The half-dozen uniformed men gathered around him. "Let's fan out and search the area." Gordon pulled out his gun. "Be careful with your firearms. Batman's out there."

He walked straight toward the building in front of him. It looked like they had finished this structure, at least on the outside. This probably would have contained the model condominium and the sales offices.

Gordon tried the front door. It was locked, and there were no broken windows or other signs of forced entry about the front of the building. He put his back to the building and held the gun close to his chest, and walked slowly to his left, watching for movement in the dark.

He turned the corner and heard somebody running. Gordon raised his gun.

"Freeze! Police!"

Batman ran out into the light.

"He's gone, Jim! He's completely disappeared." Batman scattered a pile of rubble with his boot. "It's impossible! He has to be here! He has to be!"

Gordon holstered his gun and walked quickly toward the other man. He had seldom seen Batman show any emotion, and never anything like this.

"Tell me what happened," Gordon said evenly.

The commissioner's level approach seemed to have an effect. Batman breathed deeply, and his tone was calmer when he spoke. "The moment I drove in here, the signal vanished. It's almost as if they were waiting for me——"

"No, Batman," Gordon answered quickly. "There's got to be another explanation."

"Most likely," the other man agreed. "If only I understood *any* of this."

As much at it worried him, Gordon guessed he could understand his old friend's dilemma. This case made less sense than most, and that was saying a lot in a city the size of Gotham. And why the Batman costumes? The real Batman seemed to be taking them all too personally, which, Gordon assumed, was part of the plan concocted by whoever was behind all this. Gordon was afraid that Batman was already too close to all of this. What would happen if there were any more of these murders?

"I have to get into these buildings," Batman said.

No, Gordon realized. It had to stop here. "Batman, we're stretching our authority even being on these grounds without due cause. We can't go in there. We'll have to come back in the morning with a search warrant."

Batman stared at the commissioner for a long moment. "Of course, Commissioner. You'll have to forgive me. We were getting so close."

Maybe, Gordon thought, too close.

"Batman," he said, "it's time to leave."

Gordon waited for Batman to start back to the parking lot before he followed.

"So that's Joey Droll?" Nightwing mused as Gordon stopped the tape. To his eyes, the "reverend" seemed equal parts politician, comedian, and door-to-door salesman. Nightwing couldn't see how anybody could trust somebody like that, much less devote his life to Droll's church.

"At least, that's his public image," the commissioner agreed. "We haven't been able to find out anything about his private self, or his past before he came to Gotham City. At the very least, he's dishonest. I have the feeling that his organization is very dangerous. Did Batman tell you about Thompson?"

"A little bit. He was the rookie who disappeared?"

Gordon nodded. "From the face of the earth. Once you get in there, don't trust anybody."

Nightwing stood. "Actually, Commissioner, I came here to talk about more than the Church of Perpetual Happiness."

"Batman?" Gordon asked.

It was Nightwing's turn to nod. "That's the real reason I came to work on this case. I've never seen Batman like this before."

"Nor have I," Gordon agreed. "He seems to be obsessed."

Nightwing thought about the strained exchange they had

had on the phone that morning. Batman could talk about the case with him, but nothing else.

"He blames himself for everything."

"Everything?" Gordon considered. "Whatever's going on inside his head isn't healthy." He paused, as if gauging what else he could say. "Well, now I guess we can both watch him. But don't let your worry about your old partner make you ignore the dangers of what you're about to do."

"Don't worry, sir," Nightwing replied. "I won't let you down. Batman trained me well."

Nightwing, and Dick Grayson, only hoped that Batman would remember his own training.

The signal had started to work again.

It had been close to sunset, and Bruce Wayne had been eating a light dinner. Batman was due to leave soon, in order to discreetly guard Winter at that Church of Perpetual Happiness function. Bruce had rigged his computer system to let him know if there was a signal or other unusual electronic activity, and had heard the telltale chime as he sipped his decaffeinated coffee.

He left Alfred to remove his dinner as he quickly descended to the Batcave to investigate. One look at his main color monitor told him it looked like the same signal, coming from more-or-less the same place. He couldn't tell any more until he got much closer to the current location of the device.

It only took a moment for Batman and the Batmobile to return to the road. The signal didn't waver. It seemed to be coming from the same place he had lost it the night before. But what could have interfered with it? There was always the possibility of a defect in the tracking device itself, but if it had shut off, why had it started working again? Big Mike could have passed behind lead shielding or even bedrock of sufficient thickness to cut off the signal, too. That was certainly possible, although Batman knew of no natural or man-made obstacle of that sort in all of Gotham City.

There was a third possibility as well. The device could have been tampered with. If that was the case, the signal had been set off again as a sort of invitation, and Batman might be speeding into a trap.

For the first time in weeks, Batman smiled. He'd look forward to a trap.

Gordon met a very nervous Steven Winter around the corner from the Church of Perpetual Happiness. The mayor's assistant seemed very surprised to see Gordon by himself.

"Where's Batman?" Winter asked.

"I'm sure he's around here somewhere," Gordon reassured the other man. "In cases like this, Batman is good at staying in the shadows. Besides, we'll have seven other men inside the building with you at all times, including six detectives under my direct control."

"Seven?" Winter pushed his hands in his pockets, even though the night wasn't very cold. "Who's the seventh?"

"That's right. I didn't have a chance to tell you about our important volunteer. Nightwing will be coming to our little party, too—incognito, of course."

"Nightwing?" Winter asked.

"He used to work with Batman. Now he's out on his own—except for the occasional special favor."

Winter laughed nervously. "Well, if you see him, tell him thanks from me."

"Oh, I imagine we'll both see him," Gordon tried to answer cheerfully. "We just won't know who he is."

There was a burst of static on his car radio.

"Seven-four-seven," a voice said. "We're all ready."

"Good," Gordon said to the radio. "Seven-four-seven out." He turned back to Winter. "The men are in position—three outside, three inside. I'm going to run things from here. I'm afraid my face is a little too well known for me to do any close-up undercover work."

"So," Winter said as he took his hands out of his pockets, "I guess I take it from here."

"Good luck, Steve." Gordon held out his hand. "This is a high-profile event. They're using your presence for publicity value, so I don't think you're in any real danger. Unless, I suppose, you stumble onto something they don't want you to see. Even then, I think we can protect you. But find out what you can. Any information you can get may be vital in helping us to close down this church and maybe find the missing police officer."

Gordon watched Winter walk up the street and around the corner. He didn't like the fact that he had to lie to the mayor's assistant. On this sort of a case, Batman would generally make his presence known, to Gordon at the very least. For some reason, Batman hadn't shown.

Gordon had to admit it. He was worried, and not particularly about what would happen to Winter. He figured that his men could handle almost anything that might happen. But to see no sign of Batman—he hadn't even sent a message—that could be serious.

Batman pulled into the parking lot of the half-built condominium complex. It looked exactly as it had the night before, only now the homing device was working. It flashed regularly on the small screen to the right of the steering wheel, a steady blue dot in the upper center, directly in front of the nose of the Batmobile. A digital readout printed out the range: twenty meters. Batman looked ahead. That meant it was somewhere inside that locked building.

He got out of the Batmobile. With luck, Big Mike was waiting for him.

10

Steven Winter had never felt this anxious walking into church. But then, he'd never entered a church like this before. The outside of the place certainly looked traditional enough. Winter had done some research and had discovered that the Perpetual Happiness people had purchased it from an inner-city congregation that had shrunk too much to support it.

The two great wooden doors at the top of the steps were both thrown open, allowing golden light to spill into the gathering dusk. There was music coming from the church as well, but not the traditional choir and organ sort of thing. No, this was a soprano belting out a song about the power of joy, backed by a heavy drumbeat—sort of a cross between gospel and disco.

He started up the steps.

"Why, look who's here!" someone called enthusiastically. "Reverend Droll, please come quickly!"

A man wearing robes of maroon satin stepped out of the church.

"Mr. Winter!" Joey Droll greeted him with his ever-present smile. "It is always an honor to receive a visit from an important member of city government."

Droll quickly descended the steps to shake Winter's hand. As they did so, half a dozen flash bulbs went off around them. Winter hadn't even realized there were any cameras.

Droll laughed a bit too jovially. "The press, you know. When two media figures of our stature meet, it's an historic occasion."

Media figures? Historic occasion? All the cameras seemed to be held by young people, probably church members. Wasn't the reverend laying all this on a bit thick?

The mayor's assistant found the reverend's hand firmly planted in the middle of Winter's back as he was led upstairs.

There seemed to be a party going on inside.

Dick waited until he saw the mayor's assistant enter the church. He had picked up an "invitation" to the party at Gotham State—they had a pile of copies on the table outside the cafeteria.

YOU'RE INVITED!
MEET SPECIAL MAYORAL ASSISTANT STEVEN
WINTER!
HAVE YOUR SAY ABOUT THE PROBLEMS
AFFECTING GOTHAM CITY!

REFRESHMENTS SERVED.
PRESENTED COURTESY OF
THE REVEREND JOEY DROLL
AND THE CHURCH OF PERPETUAL HAPPINESS.
PLEASE BRING THIS INVITATION.

The paper tried to imply that this invitation was something special, even though it was taken from a pile of a couple hundred of the exact same thing. And Dick had seen dozens more of the flyers, tacked to trees, lampposts, and telephone poles all around town. Droll and the church were getting all the mileage they could out of this.

But he'd better get in there after Winter. Gordon said he'd appreciate it if Dick kept an eye on the mayor's assistant. Besides that, of course, Batman wanted him to find out everything he could about the church.

Invitation in hand, Dick climbed the steps. He stepped inside the front door into a large, very crowded room.

"Hello, friend!" shouted a tall skinny man of around Dick's age as he snatched the invitation from Dick's hand. "Welcome to our little community. I assume this is your first time here?"

"Uh," Dick replied, a bit startled by the greeter's enthusiasm. "Yes."

"Well, we certainly hope it won't be your last. I'm Larry." He grabbed Dick's shoulder a bit too firmly. "And what's your name?"

Dick was ready for this part. He and Batman had decided his alias should be "Dick Brown." He gave the guy his first name.

"Wait just a second, Dick." Larry turned to scan the crowd behind him. "Sharon? Could you take a minute to show one of our new friends around?"

Well, Dick thought, it was certainly easy to get in here. He hoped, after he'd been here awhile, it wouldn't be too difficult getting back out.

The lock on the front door wasn't very sophisticated. It was probably just meant to keep kids from trashing the place. Batman had it opened in no time.

He stepped inside the door, into a small entryway with mailboxes to either side. He looked down at the palm-sized portable signal-finder he had brought with him, a smaller version of the screen he'd installed in the Batmobile. The signal was still straight ahead, maybe a dozen feet away, just on the other side of the inner door, which stood slightly ajar.

This almost seemed too easy. Was Big Mike waiting for him on the other side of the door?

Well, there was no reason for Batman to open the door personally. He pulled a custom-made boomerang from his belt, crafted with enough weight so should he throw it at the right angle, it would push the door open and show whatever was on the other side.

Batman stepped back to the door that led outside and tossed his calling card.

The boomerang banged against the handle to the inner door, throwing it open.

Explosion. The inner room was filled with blinding light and deafening noise.

Ripped from its hinges, the inner door was flying straight for him.

Winter was surrounded by members of the church. Really surrounded. Did they have to stand quite so close?

"Mr. Winter, we're so happy to meet you."

"You'll have to come to some of our special seminars."

"We'd always value your opinion."

Actually, the things people were saying were very flattering. If only it weren't quite so hot in here.

The Reverend Droll was suddenly at his elbow again. "You'll have to forgive my followers. Members of my church aren't just happy, they're enthusiastic."

Enthusiastic, Winter thought, and a little strange. Coupled with the information Gordon had given him about organizations like this church, he was becoming increasingly uneasy.

"But come," the reverend continued smoothly. "You haven't sampled our buffet." Droll led Winter away from the crowd. The same six flashes went off again. For some reason Winter thought about how members of certain primitive societies believed that having their picture taken would capture their souls.

Droll led him over to a table laden with baked goods and other sweets. "This is a special occasion, so my flock has prepared some special foods."

Winter didn't feel very hungry. There was no reason, he supposed, that the church would be out to poison him. After all, there were all those flash cameras around. Then again, food could contain subtler things than poison. And Winter doubted that those half-dozen cameras were here for anything but Reverend Droll's personal use.

No, he was being silly. Winter was an old hand at handling media events. Commissioner Gordon had been absolutely correct about that; this was a media event, and Winter was perfectly safe.

"Why," he forced himself to say, "I guess I wouldn't mind a cupcake."

"Excellent!" Reverend Droll picked up a paper plate,

decorated with a stylized smiling face, red features on a blue background. He looked over the homemade baked goods, then plucked a cupcake that was especially large and loaded with icing. "This one should be particularly tempting."

Winter smiled as he accepted the plate. Somehow, he didn't care for Droll's choice of words.

"Would you like some of our Celestial punch to help wash that down?"

Winter considered the offer as he took a bite. A bit sweet, but not bad.

"Alcohol-free, of course," Droll continued. He chuckled merrily. "We fill it instead with our own special brand of joy."

Joy? Winter didn't like the sound of that at all. What could that mean? LSD, perhaps, or some newer, even more potent concoction?

"Not just now." He forced himself to swallow, then carefully put down the plate.

"Oh, I know, it is difficult to eat when all this excitement is going on around you. And believe me, Mr. Winter, it is always exciting in the Church of Perpetual Happiness."

"I don't doubt it." Winter's voice came out as a croak. The cupcake crumbs seemed to have gotten lodged in his throat. Were there napkins around here somewhere? He spotted some, all sporting that same stylized-smile design, on the corner of the table. "Pardon me." He reached past Droll.

"Is something the matter?" the reverend asked solicitously. "We can't have any problems with our honored guests. Not good for business, ha, ha." Another pair of churchgoers hurried over to the reverend's side. "Are you sure you won't have any punch?"

Winter noticed that both of the newcomers looked like college basketball players—tall and well muscled. One of them scooped a cup of the livid pink punch and, smiling, stuck it under Winter's nose.

"Go ahead," Droll urged. "Great for the palate. And, believe me, even better for the mind."

The two basketball players pressed closer, both grinning as though they were having the best times of their lives. Winter felt like the walls were closing in.

"Can't," he choked. "Need air."

He bolted for the nearest door.

"Hi, Dick," Sharon said. "Have you ever been truly happy?"

Dick had to admit, it was a different opening line. And Sharon was a very attractive woman, slim, in her early twenties, with long blond hair and a smile that lit up her face.

"Once or twice," Dick answered. "I'm pretty happy most of the time."

"Pretty happy?" Her voice sounded the slightest bit disapproving, even though her smile was still there. "That's not really the same thing, is it?"

"Maybe not," Dick admitted. He was about to ask her what true happiness was when she impulsively grabbed his hand.

"Come on," she said as she flashed her smile again. "Let me show you some of the things our church does."

Why not? Dick thought. There were certainly worse ways to spend an evening. And as long as they stayed in the church building, he could keep a pretty good eye on Winter.

"We have a soup kitchen downstairs," she began as

she pulled him through the crowd, "for those less fortunate than ourselves. Reverend Droll wants to make sure everyone gets their needs met. That's the first step toward happiness."

Dick hated to admit it, but—at least for the time being—Sharon was making a certain amount of sense. He wondered if there really could be a formula for happiness.

"Come on, I'll show you some photos of the shelters we've set up. And our brand-new mission school!" She tugged at his hand again. "They're back here in the library." She giggled. "Reverend Droll believes in being well read."

She led him to a door at the back of the room. Dick wondered if he should follow her in there. Still, he imagined he could hear what was going on if he was only a room away.

There was a commotion behind him. He turned to see Winter running to an open door on the far side of the room.

"Something's the matter," he said.

But Sharon kept a firm grip on his hand. "I'm sure it's nothing. Some of our church members are doctors. They'll take care of any problem."

Any problem? Actually, now that Winter had run from the building, he'd be under the watchful eyes of the cops Gordon had stationed outside—and away from anything that might have happened to him in the middle of this crowd. Dick relaxed a bit.

"Dick," Sharon urged, "you don't want to leave just yet. There's so much I have to show you."

Dick guessed it was better if he stayed. He'd certainly been accepted easily enough. And maybe Sharon would show him something he could use.

He nodded and smiled himself. "Okay. Lead on."

* * *

Oh, God, he was out of there! He could hear nothing but the pounding of his heart. He crashed through the bushes behind the church, only stopping once the greenery hid him from the building.

Winter had never reacted like that before. There was just something about that church, and the reverend and his followers, and the way they never stopped smiling. That, and what Gordon had told him before. Winter had to calm down. He took a deep breath.

He heard the rustle of leaves in front of him. Was one of Gordon's detectives coming to check on him? He looked up and saw a man dressed all in black, from his face mask down to his boots. Would the police go to such an extreme measure to hide themselves?

The man in black waved to Winter.

"Come to papa," he called.

Haley was three minutes late in checking in. Gordon tried to call him on his walkie-talkie, but got no response. He called the other two men he had positioned outside.

"We have a situation here. Position Three is not responding. I need someone to check out his position."

"This is Two," the answer came back. "Will do."

Another call came in. "Six here. Winter left the church two minutes ago, running for Position Three. Four and Five are in active pursuit."

This was bad. Something had gone wrong.

"One!" he barked into the radio. "Winter is outside. Circle the church counterclockwise. I'll go the other way and meet you around back." Gordon could no longer afford to stay uninvolved. He started up his car and drove it down the street and around the corner to the church.

"Chief!" a voice, badly shaken, came on the radio. "I found—um—Three. He's been knocked cold, but he's still breathing. Four and Five are here, too. They can't find Winter anywhere. He's gone."

Commissioner Gordon swore.

Batman jumped outside the outer entryway as the inner door slammed into the mailboxes. He waited a long moment, careful of any secondary blasts, but nothing followed.

Satisfied that it was reasonably safe, he stepped back inside the entryway to the building. It had been a first-class explosion. If he had walked through that second door, he would have been blown into tiny pieces.

Jason. Not now. He pushed the thought from his mind.

He sidestepped the now-twisted metal door frame that had uprooted a half-dozen feet of carpet and linoleum, and walked through the site of the explosion. The walls and ceiling had been torn away here, leaving exposed pipes and bricks. Batman wondered what he was expecting to find.

He noticed something in the settling dust—a well-lit room at the end of the corridor. The door had been left open, just for him. Last time he had seen an open door, there was a bomb on the other side. What sort of surprise waited for him here?

He studied the corridor in front of him. The dust would have shown any light-activated alarms. The explosion would have neutralized any sonic devices. He walked cautiously down the hall, careful of trip wires and pressure plates in the floor.

But there seemed to be no other traps; only the warm, welcoming light of the open door.

He stopped again at the threshold. The room on the other side was bare, except for a single, small wooden table. On that table were a half-dozen flowers, shaped like pale yellow roses, but made of colored paper—the same roses they sold at the Church of Perpetual Happiness. And next to the artificial roses was an unopened deck of cards, its seal still intact.

Batman couldn't help but feel these objects had been left here for him; his reward for having survived the bomb blast. Or perhaps whoever left these items knew Batman was too smart to fall for the bomb, and had left the explosives there to get rid of any casual intruders.

Batman knew that was the way his adversary thought. He knew who he was fighting, now, but he opened the cards anyway. After all, his adversary would want him to.

As he expected, every card in the pack was a joker.

Jason, Batman thought.

PART II

You Don't Mind
a Little Joke?

11

This was just *too* funny for words.

Samson had stolen a mayor's assistant for him from right under the noses of Gordon and his meddling police. And right out beyond the back door of that wonderful Church of Perpetual Happiness, too! It had been very considerate of the church to make such a big deal out of Winter's visit. It had made Samson's job so much easier.

And now Steven Winter waited in one of The Joker's specially prepared cells.

The mayor's assistant was still sound asleep, of course, thanks to the drugs they had given him. The drugs were a very important part of the treatment. The Joker gazed fondly at the sleeping Winter's form on video monitor number four—so innocent, so peaceful, so ready to begin. The Joker giggled.

"I'm glad you're having such a good time," Samson said dryly. "But aren't you forgetting something?"

The Joker sighed. Such a pity. Underlings. They could be so annoying. But they had their place, even though Samson seemed to be forgetting his. And he was too good at his job, at least so far, for The Joker to give him any of those very special reminders. The Joker chuckled.

Ah, if only he had had a gang full of Samsons, The Joker would have taken over Gotham City by now. Instead, he had a gang full of Big Mikes, who blew museum jobs and ran away without any of the loot. Oh, the things he had to put up with!

Now, he might be able to do something interesting with Big Mike. The Joker cackled.

There was a time and a place for everything.

This was the place, but what was the time? The Joker checked his watch. The mouse's hands said that their new guest should be waking up ever so soon.

"I'm waiting," Samson remarked.

Waiting? The Joker could fix that very easily. Samson would never have to wait again.

No. No, no. Samson was too good at his job. A time and a place, he remembered.

The Joker smiled instead. "First," he said pleasantly, "I have to check the merchandise."

He glanced back at the video monitor and pressed the large button with the happy face. The siren blared over Winter's bed as the bank of floodlights made the room brighter than a desert at noon.

Winter jumped from his bed. "What? Who?" He stumbled groggily, those lovely drugs still gurgling through his system. The poor mayor's assistant! He had to lean against the bars to keep his balance. He blinked, trying to focus. "What's going on—"

Ah. Mr. Winter was trying to talk in coherent sentences. That would never do. The Joker pressed the next button over, the one he liked to think of as the "joy buzzer."

Winter screamed as any number of volts of electricity flowed from the metal bars into his body. Oh, not enough to kill him, certainly, but enough for him to remember.

Soon, the electricity would be virtually the only thing he could remember.

The Joker pulled his thumb off the buzzer. Winter fell to his knees with a groan, a sound more animal than human.

The Joker clapped. Ah, this was working better with each victim. What a brilliant plan! Of course, only a genius like The Joker could have conceived it.

It had all come to him one afternoon as he was considering his rather dramatic fate—how the meddling Batman had caused him to fall into a pool of toxic chemicals, and how it had changed his appearance, and his outlook, forever.

He should thank Batman, really. The costumed clown's interference transformed him, leading him from a life of ordinary crime to an even better life of extraordinary crime. Of course, he'd like to thank that freak in a very *special* way.

He paused for a moment to admire himself in the mirror he always kept handy. The bright green hair, the dead-white skin, the bloodred lips. What a striking face! It did nothing less than set a new standard for beauty—and it was The Joker's duty to make the world recognize that standard.

Batman-Batman-Batman—he was more than just a creep with a cape. He had to be to best The Joker. When The Joker had thought about it in one of his rare moments of leisure, he had realized that Batman and The Joker weren't like ordinary men—they had special lives. To have different faces, and different identities; my, that sort of thing didn't happen to just anybody. And that was such a shame.

But—and this was The Joker's wonderful idea—it *could* happen to anybody, with a little help. Now, The Joker was unique. It would take real work to come up with somebody else anywhere nearly as special. But Batman? Heck, he was just some guy in a costume! Maybe, The Joker had realized, it was time to make Batman a little less unique.

He did have a bit of a grudge against the costumed fellow, anyway. Batman had this annoying habit of surviving The Joker's little traps. And on top of that, Batman got all the lucky breaks! Look at the facts! How many times had he captured The Joker at the very instant The Joker was about to escape? What were the odds against that sort of thing? It was uncanny. Batman must have had a rabbit's foot built into his cowl, four-leaf clovers jammed into his futility belt. Who ever heard of a lucky bat?

And then, to add insult to injury, the caped creep had the temerity to put The Joker behind bars!

Well, The Joker had finally figured out a way to make Batman's luck run out.

That was his special idea. Maybe The Joker couldn't kill the Batman just yet. But what if he could train any number of new batmen? He could kidnap likely recruits right under the noses of the authorities, and make bat freaks of his very own!

He could start winning. He could kill Batman over and

over again, while putting in important practice time for killing the real thing. Talk about the best of both worlds! Sometimes even The Joker couldn't believe how clever he was.

Samson cleared his throat.

Oh, dear. The Joker had been spending a wee bit of time gloating, hadn't he? But, then again, when you were as clever as certain Jokers, you deserved time to gloat!

"Oh, yes, the money," he murmured happily. He pulled a "Welcome Steve Winter" flyer from the top of the pile. It was awfully thoughtful of that church to print so many of them; they made great scrap paper. He pulled out his pen and wrote down a figure in purple ink.

"Take this down to Big Mike," The Joker said as he handed the flyer to Samson. "He'll give you what's coming to you. Oh, and count the money yourself. Poor Big Mike has a little trouble with addition."

Samson smiled when he saw the number The Joker had written. It included a bit of a bonus. Winter, after all, was such a prime specimen, Samson deserved a little extra. And, heaven knew, these days The Joker had enough money to toss around. Yes, The Joker could be generous in so many ways.

Samson turned and left. Now The Joker could get down to serious business.

"Let me out of here!" Winter yelled. Oh, my. He had recovered enough to notice the video monitor. "Do you know who I am? You'll pay for this!"

What wonderful outrage. What a good Batman this one would make.

What could The Joker do but laugh?

12

Much too late the Batmobile slid silently in behind Gordon's unmarked car. Gordon and the other detectives stood and watched as the cockpit popped open and Batman jumped out.

"I was called away on other business," Batman said as he approached. "Has Winter gone inside?"

"He's come, and he's gone." Gordon explained what had happened—at least what little they knew about it.

Batman's face paled under the mask. Gordon realized that, especially in the state Batman was now in, his friend would hold himself responsible for Winter's disappearance, even though Batman wasn't present at the scene of the abduction.

"There's no way to know if you could have stopped it," Gordon cautioned.

"I could have," Batman replied simply. "Somebody

wanted me out of the way, lured me back to the place where I'd lost Big Mike the night before. They led me straight to a bomb.''

A bomb? Gordon frowned. What was Batman trying to tell him?

"Meant for me. I wasn't hurt," Batman continued. "The main building of the complex lost a few bricks and a lot of plaster. But once I'd gotten through the dust, I noticed our adversary had left us a little present.''

"Our adversary?" Gordon asked.

Batman handed him a deck of cards. When Gordon looked inside, he saw that every card was a joker.

"But he can't be—" Gordon began, then stopped himself. The Joker had escaped from prisons and mental institutions, even seemingly come back from the dead, more times than the commissioner could remember. Sometimes, it seemed there was little The Joker *couldn't* do.

Gordon decided to ask a question instead. "So The Joker's behind all this? Then you're implying that he left the cards there on purpose. Why would he announce himself like that?''

"Why does The Joker do anything?" Batman answered. "You can be sure it's part of some sort of warped plan. Beyond that, we don't have enough information to go on.''

"Wait a moment," Detective Ianella interjected. "What about Winter's kidnapping? Is this church involved? Or does The Joker only want us to think that to throw us off the trail? I don't get any of this.''

Batman nodded curtly as he turned to look at the church building. "That's The Joker's plan. The Joker bores easily. He needs these elaborate plots to keep his interest. That's why he makes this all so tantalizing, the same way a spider builds a glittering web to catch a fly.''

"So The Joker is taunting us?" Ianella asked.

Batman turned back to the detective. "He's raising the stakes. We now know that The Joker is involved, but how does that help us? In a way, it only makes us more concerned, since we know the crazed and deadly lengths The Joker can go to." He balled both his hands into fists. "But I think, really, The Joker needs us to be chasing him. His crimes only have meaning for him when he's being pursued by the law"—he paused to stare down at his fists—"and Batman."

Commissioner Gordon never ceased to be astonished by how well Batman could read his adversaries' motives. Everything Batman said seemed to reflect The Joker's patterns—and Gordon knew from experience that all of The Joker's schemes always exhibited a weird logic of their own, almost as if the criminal relied on the pattern of his crimes to give him some semblance of sanity.

But then, Gordon reflected, as much as a villain like the Joker needed Batman as a constant foil—Batman, on some level, seemed to respond to the challenge of the Joker in kind. They both seemed to do their best when they faced each other, strangely equal on opposite sides of the law.

"That may be The Joker's real reason," Batman admitted. "He wants to draw me in. He's already killed Robin. He wants me to be next.

"Where did Winter disappear?"

Flashlight in hand, Gordon led the way back to the dense undergrowth behind the Church of Perpetual Happiness. Batman and two of his detectives followed. There wasn't anything resembling a path back here, but Gordon tried to march across the most trampled patches of grass to keep from destroying any more evidence.

He stopped at the base of a large tree. "This is where

we found Detective Haley. According to the doctor, he suffered a blow to the back of the head. He regained consciousness as they loaded him on the ambulance. Said he didn't see a thing.'' Gordon stopped and swore under his breath. "There must be something we can find!"

"Sounds like a professional," Batman commented. He pointed down at the crushed grass. "The ambulance attendants had to come through here?"

"And all the others, too," Gordon agreed. "Me and the detectives, along with a couple of the people from the church. That's where the doctor came from."

"Not much left to go on," Batman said as he studied the area to either side of the trampled path. He moved out of the flashlight's beam. "Commissioner! Over here!"

Gordon followed Batman, bringing his flashlight with him.

Batman pointed. "Show the beam over there."

Gordon swept the light across the ground. There, a few inches in front of Batman's boots, was a deep foot impression, sinking not only through the grass, but leaving a heel impression in the earth.

"These imprints are much deeper than any of the others," Batman pointed out. "This man was carrying somebody else—see the depth of the heel mark there?—while he was backing up to turn around."

"Right," Gordon agreed. "We've got our kidnapper. Ianella? Get an impression of that boot print there, and anything else you can find."

"Right away," Ianella agreed, trotting back out to the cruisers.

"But where could the kidnapper have gone?" Detective Garcia pointed out. "At most, he had a two-minute window to get out of here."

Gordon glanced up at Batman. "Let's find out, shall we?"

The footsteps turned around about four yards beyond the tree, and soon led to a dirt road.

Gordon grunted as he looked at the tire tracks. "It's a fire road. The whole area back here had them before the developers moved in." He looked up at the remaining detective. "Garcia? Get Ianella to get an impression of this tire when he's done with the shoes, would you?" He glanced at Batman. "Anything else you want to look at?"

"It'll be hard to see anything more in the dark," the other man said softly. "You'll sweep the area after daylight. Let me know if you find anything." Batman paused in thought. "Do you have any idea why Winter left the church in such a hurry?"

"None that makes any sense," Gordon replied. "The doctor from the church thought it might have been some sort of claustrophobic reaction. Of course, I don't know how much we can trust a report from a church member."

Batman coughed softly. "We had other people in the church."

Gordon shook his head. "My detectives weren't close enough to hear the conversation. Winter was over by the refreshment table, surrounded by the Reverend Droll and half a dozen church members; the noise level was too high to make out much of anything."

Batman looked at Gordon. "And Nightwing?"

Did Gordon notice some extra tension in Batman's voice? After all this time, the commissioner thought he could detect his friend's moods, despite the mask. This mood seemed none too positive.

"Nightwing hasn't contacted us," Gordon replied neutrally. "We assume he's still inside."

That seemed to satisfy Batman. When he spoke again,

the coldness was gone. Maybe, Gordon realized, Batman was afraid that Nightwing might die as well.

"Good," Batman said. "He can tell us if anything did go wrong in there. Or if there's any other connection between The Joker and the church."

Gordon admired Batman's faith in his former sidekick. He just hoped it wasn't misplaced. Gordon had already lost two men because of the Church of Perpetual Happiness.

He prayed to all that was holy that it wouldn't become three.

Sharon's hand was on top of his own. He could feel her breath on the side of his neck.

"Don't worry," she said, her voice little more than a whisper. "The church can handle this. We get these sorts of disturbances all the time."

She was so close, she made the hairs stick up on the back of Dick's neck. She smelled of soap and shampoo, sweet, common smells that on her somehow became warm, and attractive. Her blond hair had a tendency to fall in front of her green eyes, and she wrinkled her nose every time she pushed it out of the way. She smiled at him. How could this church be so bad if it brought out that sort of smile?

But, somehow, with this other woman so close, he couldn't help thinking about Kory. Why had they fought so much? Why did he really feel he had to move out? Had he lost Kory forever?

"Something's bothering you," Sharon said with sudden concern.

"Well," Dick replied, "life hasn't exactly been easy lately."

"Then you've come to the right place. It is only through the church that any of us can find true happiness." She grabbed him firmly by the arm and led him out of the main room.

Dick almost pulled away. What if Winter was in serious trouble? But he reminded himself that Batman and the others should handle that. He was doing his job, and from the way he was so readily accepted, he seemed to be doing it well.

Sharon led him down a long corridor, lit only by small light bulbs, every twenty feet or so. Dick hadn't realized how large this building was. He wondered how many church members it really held?

"You saw what happened out there, didn't you?" Sharon said as they walked. "The authorities don't trust us. There were plainclothes detectives in our church, watching everything we said to our distinguished guest. We were surrounded by police. All our church wants to do is bring happiness to our world, and to Gotham City. But they can't believe in the purity of our vision."

"Well," Dick pointed out, "Winter is an important man—"

"And we're an important church!" Sharon retorted. "I'm sorry, but if Reverend Droll could get one-tenth the respect that some of these politicians receive—" She paused in front of a door. "Do you hear voices?"

Dick frowned. They had passed close to a dozen doors as they had talked, and each one had looked exactly like the closed door now in front of them, a new coat of white paint shining dully underneath the fifteen-watt bulb.

Sharon opened the door, and Dick could hear a number of voices engaged in spirited conversation.

"Tom!" Sharon called reprovingly. "What are you doing in here? You're going to miss the party!"

A tall fellow with a scraggly beard smiled and shrugged. "This is the night for our study group. I always meet with our study group."

The twenty-odd people crammed in the room all waved and shouted hello.

Sharon laughed delightedly, then turned to Dick. "I'm afraid Tom's a lot closer to true happiness than I am. If everybody were like Tom, Reverend Droll would have converted all of Gotham City by now!" She squeezed the place where she still held Dick's arm. "Say, I have an idea! You want to learn more about what we do, don't you? What better way to learn than to sit in on Tom's study group?"

Dick smiled uncertainly. He thought he was going to get a chance to look around the church building. Well, he supposed it could wait a little while. Still, there was something about this room, with so many people in so little space. What was this study group thing all about? One minute, Sharon and he were talking, the next he seemed to have been surrounded by church members.

Sharon closed the door behind them.

13

"Mr. Winter?"

He woke with a jolt. He had been dreaming of being trapped in a deep hole with no light, and no air, and no way out.

"Mr. Winter? Please."

Steve Winter opened his eyes. He had trouble focusing. Where was he? There were two shapes in front of him. He blinked. Two men, he thought.

"Mr. Winter?" the voice addressed him again. It seemed to carry a slight foreign accent that Winter couldn't identify. "You will address me as Dr. Andrews."

No. Winter was an assistant to the mayor. Whatever was going on here, he was having none of it. He tried to stand up. Something was keeping his arms and legs from moving too far. He stared down at his right arm. There was a metal bracelet of some sort there, a bracelet and a chain.

"What the hell is going on here?" Winter demanded.

He screamed as fire shot up his arms and legs, and collapsed back on the bunk behind him.

"No disrespect, now," Dr. Andrews remarked. "You will receive a disciplinary jolt whenever you show disrespect. Now address me properly."

Winter blinked again. His eyes were finally coming into focus. One of the men before him seemed awfully pale.

"The hell I—" he began.

His body was wracked again by fire.

"Please, Mr. Winter," the first man said. "We do not wish to damage you beyond repair. My name, please?"

Winter gasped for breath. "Dr.—Dr. Andrews."

"That's much better," Andrews replied. "And see how much better everything is when you cooperate?"

Winter nodded quickly, not wishing to feel the fire again.

"That's right," Andrews continued in the same unctuous tone. "All our guests learn to play along sooner or later."

"What—" Winter asked tentatively. There was no jolt of electricity. "What do you want?"

"We will ask the questions," Andrews answered. "You will not be punished this time, because you did not know the rules. For now, you will only speak when you are spoken to. But you haven't met out real host. Without him, Mr. Winter, all this would not be possible. Why don't you say thank you to Mr. Joker?"

Joker? The name went through Winter with close to the same force as the electricity. He blinked again, and his eyes suddenly focused on a pair of red lips twisted into the caricature of a smile.

The Joker was behind all this? For the first time, Winter realized he had no hope.

"Mr. Winter?" Andrews prompted.

"Thank you—Mr. Joker," Winter managed.

The Joker clapped his gloved hands together. "Excellent! You may have some doubts about us at first, Mr. Winter, but sooner or later, you'll find it *very* cozy. Like a home away from home." His smile widened to show his teeth. "Trust me."

The Joker started to laugh. Winter wanted to cry. But he wouldn't. He was too afraid of the shock.

Dr. Andrews waited until they had closed the door on the cell block before he pulled out a cigarette. It was better when dealing with a new subject that you did not show him any of your weaknesses. If was better if you barely showed you were human at all.

He lit the cigarette with his silver lighter, one of the few objects he had kept from his past, and took a long, slow puff of the superior American tobacco.

The Joker looked amused. But then, The Joker always looked amused.

Andrews pulled the cigarette from his lips and stared at the smoke rising toward the air vent. "I am glad you are giving me better specimens."

His employer waved away any thanks Andrews might offer with a brushing motion of both his hands. "I promised you, didn't I? The Joker is always true to his word." He grunted comically. "And after the money I paid to get you over here, why wouldn't I want you to have the best materials?"

Andrews nodded. This was all working out quite pleasantly. "Mr. Winter is younger and stronger than the others. We can do more with him, and more quickly."

"I simply felt it was a shame to waste your talents," The Joker replied graciously.

"Talents!" The smoke tasted suddenly bitter against the doctor's tongue. "They used my abilities for years, in some of the finest psychiatric hospitals available. Until, of course, these new freedoms started to get the better of my countrymen, and they began looking to find scapegoats for their perceived misdoings! And just as I developed my new drug! What I could have done, if they had only given me the chance. The fools have never known what's good for them!"

Andrews took a deep breath. He had to calm down. There was no need to dwell on the past. He puffed again on his cigarette and glanced over at The Joker. "I understand your own government no longer allows such important experiments anymore. They are all shortsighted fools!"

The Joker giggled at the other man's outburst. "I've *always* said the same thing. That's why you've had to move to the private sector, Andropov. Oh, so sorry Dr. Andrews. I have any number of ways for you to experiment with your new drug. Stick with me, and you'll learn *all* about free enterprise."

"Any number of ways?" Andrews looked at his employer with a renewed interest. "You want to do more than perfect your Batman?"

"Oh, certainly. I have experiments you haven't even dreamed of yet!" The Joker tossed his head back and laughed.

Andrews went back to smoking his cigarette. His life

had been so uncertain for the last few years. After working for the supreme rulers of his homeland, and a few terrorist leaders in various third world countries, he had been afraid he would have to make some unpleasant compromises when he had been forced to flee to the States. But The Joker made him feel right at home—a place where Andrews could do everything he desired.

Big Mike was unhappy.

It was not his fault that the museum job hadn't worked. The real Batman had shown up. Big Mike would like to see what all the other guys did when the real Batman showed up. And Big Mike had gotten away! His boss should like him for that, right?

Then why wasn't The Joker giving him anything to do? Well, he was watching the safe. The boss had told him to do that, saying, "Big Mike, watch the safe. Make sure it doesn't go anywhere." Before that, Big Mike hadn't even known the safe could move.

But the other guys were laughing at him. Samson had just come down here, with a piece of paper from the boss. The paper had a big number on it. The boss had never paid Big Mike like that when he had gone out to get the batmen! But he did pay Samson. And Big Mike had to give him the money, but he did not have to be happy about it. Especially the way Samson smiled, like he knew how good he was, and how Big Mike could not go out and get a new Batman anymore.

It made Big Mike mad.

But Big Mike still gave Samson the money. He didn't want to make another mistake like the museum. The boss did not like mistakes. But Big Mike didn't like the way Samson laughed when he walked out of the room.

Big Mike couldn't wait anymore. He didn't like to sit when other guys got to go out and do jobs for the boss. Big Mike wanted to do something real important. He had to go talk to the boss. He made sure the safe was locked and the alarm was on, and walked upstairs to the boss's office.

He could hear the boss laughing inside. He knocked on the door.

"What?" his boss yelled. "Interruptions! Interruptions!" The boss paused, then sang sweetly: "Come in!"

Big Mike opened the door.

The doctor was there. Big Mike didn't like the way the doctor looked at him. But he had to talk to the boss.

"Well," the boss demanded, "what is it?"

Part of Big Mike was sorry he had come up here. He wanted to run back to where he sat next to the safe and never move again. But the other part of him wanted to do something important, something as important as what Samson did. Big Mike remembered the way he had felt when he was back down sitting next to the safe. He had to talk.

"Boss," he began, trying hard to pick just the right words. "I been thinking."

"Really?" the boss prompted.

"I been sitting down and watching the safe," Big Mike said faster. Now that he had got started, he wanted to get it over with. "I know you told me it was an important job, but I can do more, too. You remember when Big Mike used to go and get batmen for you? Big Mike wants to do something like that again. Big Mike wants to do something important."

"Important?" The boss really smiled. Big Mike must have said the right thing. He turned to the doctor. "We have our next experiment."

"Experiment?" Big Mike asked. He didn't like the sound of that word.

"That means we're going to give you a try," the boss explained. He patted Big Mike on the back. "Big Mike, you're right. We haven't even begun to use you to your full potential."

Big Mike smiled. He was glad it was working out so well.

"That's the ticket!" the boss told him. "We're going to make you really happy!"

"What do you want Big Mike to do?" he asked.

The boss considered this for a minute. "Well, first you have to go into the cell block."

In with the prisoners? Big Mike wasn't so sure he liked that. A lot of the new batmen would blame him for catching them. But he wanted to do something important. Maybe the boss would make him a guard. That was important.

"Into the cell block," Big Mike repeated, making sure he could understand.

"That's right," the boss agreed.

"Then what?" Big Mike asked.

"I'll talk to you over the loudspeaker system," the boss told him. "I'll tell you just what to do."

"Okay," Big Mike agreed. This would be important. The boss said it would make him happy.

He walked across the room, careful not to look at the doctor, and opened the door that led to the cells.

"Good, Big Mike, good," the boss called after him. "You won't regret this."

He closed the door behind him. "What should Big Mike do now?"

"You see that empty cell at the end of the row?" his boss's voice answered from the speakers in the ceiling.

Big Mike saw it. He nodded.

"Walk over to it."

Big Mike walked. The cell door was open.

"Now walk inside."

The boss wanted him to go inside? Did he want Big Mike to clean out the cell? That wasn't as important a job as being a guard.

Big Mike went inside.

"Now slam the door."

Big Mike did what the boss said. The door shut with a clang.

"Test the door. Is it locked?"

Big Mike shook the door. It wouldn't budge.

"Yeah," Big Mike said. "The door is locked."

"Now sit down and wait for us," his boss said. "Don't worry. We won't be long."

The boss's voice cut off from the speaker in the middle of a laugh.

Big Mike sat. He did not understand.

How was this going to make Big Mike happy?

The Joker stopped laughing when he saw how urgently the doctor watched him.

"Excuse me?" the doctor interjected, pointing at The Joker with his cigarette. "But what experiment are you talking about?"

"It has occurred to me," The Joker replied slowly, savoring every syllable of his brilliant idea, "that what we are doing—fascinating though it is—might become very one-sided, producing nothing but Batman after Batman. After all, we don't want to become predictable. We need to start working on a real work of art." He paused for a moment for ultimate effect. "We need to make another me!"

"Fascinating," Dr. Andrews agreed. As he should. Who, after all, could be more fascinating than The Joker? "So we brainwash someone to think they are you? Excellent! The research can be much more exact. There will be none of the conjecture we were forced into with Batman. Yes, we should be able to be even more successful in our training." He paused to take a nervous pull on his cigarette. "But tell me, why start with Big Mike?"

The Joker shrugged. "This is new, this is experimental. Big Mike was available. And one thing about Big Mike —he's expendable."

"Good." The doctor stubbed out his cigarette in the ashtray. "I will begin work at once."

"By all means." The Joker shook his head at the enormity of all they had before them. "We are falling behind. You know, we've lost two of our recruits, and only gained one. By my reckoning, that still leaves us one Batman short."

That only made the doctor smile even more. "Indeed? Do you have any ideas?"

The doctor didn't even have to ask that question. The Joker never ran out of ideas. He studied his gloved hand as he mused: "Oh, I think that this time we should go outside politics, and into society. Somebody no one would ever consider as Batman material. Someone like a millionaire playboy."

He turned back to Andrews. "Tell me, Doctor, have you ever heard of Bruce Wayne?"

14

They had been in this room an awfully long time. It seemed like hours by now. Dick didn't want to be so rude as to glance at his watch. He wanted to be accepted by these people, after all. Still, he wished they'd get to the point of their discussion.

At first, he had listened eagerly to everything they were saying, hoping to find something in their talk about happiness that he could use. But he had realized, as he listened, that he might be looking for more than simple specifics about the workings of the group. Part of him wished that there really was some truth in their doctrines, something he himself could use to really *be* happier.

But, for all their talk, there seemed to be very few specifics. Their leader quoted long passages from the work on Reverend Droll, sometimes reflecting on why people laughed at certain events, at other times beseeching the followers to find happiness in the things around them. Dick actually thought the whole thing was a little bit too simplistic. He could be happy when he saw a flower without this group having to tell him to do so. Besides which, if you spent all your time in small intense groups like this, when would you ever get a chance to see flowers?

"I don't think our newest member is following the discussion," Sharon said softly.

Dick turned his attention back to the group. Had his disinterest been that obvious? Dick blinked and suppressed a yawn. If only it weren't so crowded and hot in this place.

"I'm sorry," he said as he shifted his position on the floor. His right leg felt as if it was falling asleep. "I guess I didn't get much sleep last night. Maybe if I could go outside for a minute and stretch my legs—"

"I know what our newcomer's problem is," the group leader said with a deep grin. "Dick, isn't it? Well, Dick, all the rest of us here are pretty advanced in the doctrine of our church. I should have realized that you probably would have no idea about some of the fine points of our discussion. But we can change that right now." He turned his beaming countenance to the others in the room, who took up every bit of furniture and floor. "I think we need to personalize this meeting a bit more, to bring Dick in and really get to know him. What do you say, gang?"

Everybody cheered.

"Good to know you, Dick!" a young man across the room shouted.

"It was tough for all of us at first," Sharon said with a smile.

"Yeah," said another woman to Sharon's left. "But it gets better all the time!"

Most of the group laughed at that, as if it were the punchline to some common joke.

"You see, Dick," the leader explained with his continuous smile, "for you to understand how we work here, we have to find out one thing about you." He pointed a long, bony index finger at the middle of Dick's face. "What's keeping you from being really happy?"

"Yeah!" came the chorus of voices from around the room. "Tell us! Tell us your problems and they'll go away!"

Dick struggled to think. One minute, he was half asleep, the next he was the center of attention. Still, he couldn't think of a better opportunity to be accepted by the group. What could he tell them? Certainly not the whole truth about Batman or Starfire and Nightwing of the Titans. But maybe he could tell them a little bit about a father figure who had shut him out, and a girlfriend who couldn't understand. Yeah. Why not?

What harm could it do?

Bruce Wayne was exhausted. And there was still so much more to do—now that he knew The Joker was involved. But how far did The Joker's involvement reach?

Was The Joker running the Church of Perpetual Happiness? Or was he just throwing extra suspicion toward an already questionable organization, to cover for those things that really were part of his plots.

No, Bruce told himself. It was too late to even ask questions. Batman's cape and mask were put back in their place in the cave beneath the mansion, and Batman's concerns had to stay there with them. Bruce Wayne had to stop sometime. Even Batman couldn't live without sleep.

He heard a familiar, discreet cough behind him. Alfred was still up at this hour?

The butler nodded as Bruce turned to face him. He held out a small envelope on a silver tray.

"Sir?" Alfred remarked. "This came in your absence."

Bruce took the envelope with a murmured thank you, then tore it open. He pulled out what looked like a printed invitation.

> The Board of Directors of the
> Gotham Fish Company
> Invite You to Join Us
> For a Discussion
> That Will Be to Our Mutual Advantage
> This Friday
> at our River Street Warehouse
> 7 P.M.

In the bottom corner were the initials R.S.V.P. and a phone number. What could this mean? When a man had as much money as Bruce Wayne, people used every device imaginable to gain his attention. And as devices went, an invitation to a fish warehouse was certainly up there with the strangest.

Alfred coughed politely once again. "Are the contents of the envelope—unusual, sir?"

Bruce looked back up at his butler and friend. "Why do you ask, Alfred?"

"Because the manner in which the envelope was delivered was not at all ordinary," the butler supplied with the slightest of wry smiles. "I felt it was worth bringing this to your attention."

"So you didn't stay up far past your usual bedtime to

hand me a social invitation?'' Bruce glanced down again at the very strange card.

"As much as I am concerned about the quality of your social life," the butler replied dryly, "no. The card was delivered late this afternoon, by a tall gentleman wearing a chauffeur's uniform and dark glasses. It was, however, the automobile the gentleman was driving that was of the greatest interest."

"And that automobile was?" prompted Bruce.

"A golden Rolls Royce, bearing a two-letter inscription on its license plate. The two letters were H and A."

"Ha?" Bruce inquired.

"Indeed," Alfred replied. "Ha."

HA? It was too obvious, which, of course, was the whole point. Bruce handed the card back to the butler. "Take a look at this, Alfred. It's an invitation to a fish-processing plant, delivered to me in a gold Rolls. Does that bring anything to mind?"

"Um." Alfred studied the card for an instant before replying. "Gold—fish, sir?"

"Exactly," Bruce replied. "A bit sarcastic, wouldn't you say? It sounds like The Joker to me."

Alfred returned his gaze to the card before him. "So this is a clue? Still, begging your pardon, sir, but why would The Joker be sending a clue to Bruce Wayne?"

"Because an ordinary citizen like Bruce Wayne wouldn't see The Joker's reference. This clue was meant to be discovered by Batman, after Bruce Wayne had visited the warehouse and disappeared."

"You don't say, sir." Alfred handed back the card. "And what does Bruce Wayne intend to do with this invitation?"

"Oh, Bruce Wayne fully plans to attend." He smiled

at his butler. "You do tell me that I don't get out enough, Alfred."

Winter jumped from his cot. From the loudness of that horn, it sounded like a Mac truck was screaming through his cell.

"What?" he yelled, too sleepy to think. "What time is it?"

"Rise and shine and greet the morning!" The Joker yelled from the other side of the bed. "It's 3:42 A.M., time for all good prisoners to get what's coming to them!"

Winter cringed. Without thinking, he had spoken back to The Joker.

Five times they had come to him in his cell, and all five times his body had been wracked with pain. He waited, trying somehow to be ready for it. But there was no electricity, no searing agony spreading from his manacles.

And yet, The Joker had spoken about "what's coming to him." Winter had become very sensitive to what The Joker spoke about.

"Winter." The Joker stood there for a moment and smiled.

Here it was. The Joker was just waiting a minute this time before he started. Winter held his breath.

"It's time for a little talk." The Joker removed an elaborate key ring from his belt and inserted a key in the lock to Winter's cell. The Joker had never opened his cell before.

"It's time to take off the kid gloves." The door swung inward, and the Joker walked into the cell. Winter didn't like The Joker inside his cell.

"It's time to get up close and personal." The Joker

strode toward him. His bright red smile was so wide, Winter thought it might devour him. Winter stumbled back onto his cot and tried to hide his face behind his hands.

"Come now, Mr. Winter," The Joker said in that same jovial tone he used no matter what he was saying. "You can run but you cannot hide, especially from your own death."

His death? Winter removed his hands. The Joker held a very large revolver.

"We've decided we have no more use for Mr. Winter," The Joker continued, pointing the gun at the other man's forehead. "Upkeep costs are so prohibitive; you know, food, electricity, maintenance. And those cleaning costs! We have to cut back where we can. No hard feelings."

Winter stared at The Joker. They were going to kill him because he cost too much to feed? But they hadn't fed him anything except drugs. Winter almost smiled. He'd be glad to volunteer to stop taking drugs.

"You don't seem to be reacting to this with the proper concern, Mr. Winter," The Joker continued. "Perhaps you think this is another one of my jokes. I assure you—"

The Joker turned the gun and pulled the trigger. The explosion was deafening in the enclosed space as the bullet whizzed past Winter's ear.

"—this is no joke," The Joker concluded. His voice sounded very far away after the strength of the explosion.

Winter just stood and stared. This had gone too far. He no longer knew how to react, even to the end of his own existence.

The Joker placed the muzzle of the revolver against the center of Winter's forehead.

"Say your prayers, Mr. Winter. I do so like to hear a man's dying prayers."

To his surprise, Winter realized he had one prayer. He prayed it would be easier after he was dead.

The Joker pulled the trigger.

15

So Mr. Bruce Wayne, or rather his alter ego Batman, would go and face The Joker again? Alfred did wish that his employer would get some rest before he attempted something like that, but he had spent too many years in Mr. Wayne's service to hope that he would take the more sensible course when it came to someone like The Joker. And ever since the unfortunate death of Master Todd, both Mr. Wayne and the Batman had been increasingly difficult.

Still, he could not let Mr. Wayne go before he had all the information.

"Is there anything else, Alfred?" Mr. Wayne asked. They both knew, if there hadn't been other matters, Alfred would have disappeared by now.

"I took the liberty to speak briefly with your accountant concerning the fish company," he replied. "Birnbridge says they have shown an amazing profit since their recent change in ownership.''

''Change in ownership?'' Mr. Wayne seemed suddenly awake. ''Now this, Alfred, is interesting.''

Alfred almost wished he didn't have to tell his employer these things. ''Sir, if I might make a respectful suggestion. Your invitation is not until the day after tomorrow. It is very late at night, and I imagine we could both do with some rest.''

Mr. Wayne nodded impatiently. ''You're right as usual, Alfred. Perhaps, after I go into the den and spend a moment with the computers—'' He paused. ''Oh. I suppose you did check on that license plate.''

''Yes, sir. That was the final thing I had to tell you.'' And something Alfred probably should have told his employer immediately. He was letting his concern for Mr. Wayne color his responsibilities. ''You'll find this most interesting. The license plate HA is registered to the Reverend Joey Droll.''

Mr. Wayne turned and was gone, straight to his computer files.

Alfred knew that his employer would get no sleep tonight.

After Dick stopped talking, other people brought up their troubles in the outside world, long involved confessions that made Dick's brief explanation seem like nothing at all.

But still the meeting didn't end.

Dick felt his eyes closing. People no longer seemed to be talking in complete sentences. They'd start and stop in the middle of thoughts, suddenly laughing for no reason. Dick realized he must be dozing off for a moment here, an instant there. He wished he didn't have to sit cross-legged, jammed between two other people. He wished it weren't so hot in here. He shook his head slowly, trying to clear it. It was like he wasn't quite asleep, but he couldn't quite wake up either.

He had to get up. He had to get out of here. He hadn't learned a single thing so far that would be useful to Batman. He'd make up some excuse, and come back and talk with these people later.

"Excuse me." He tried to stand. His legs, crossed and folded for hours, didn't want to support his weight. "I have to get out of here for a little while."

"Oh, no, Dick!" Sharon said. Her face was full of concern. How could she still be awake after so long? "It's important to stay."

Dick wondered if she could be right, if they were about to get to some point that would make all of this clear. He decided he didn't care. By staying in this meeting as long as he had, he'd shown he was interested. Surely, they could talk to him tomorrow as easily as today.

"Sorry," he managed. His voice was slurring. "Have to go."

Other members of the group leaned toward him.

"You can't leave us."

"You've come so far already."

"You need to learn the Joke."

The Joke? What was the Joke? No, Dick couldn't let himself be distracted anymore. He had to walk around until he'd cleared his head.

He managed to stand at last. A couple of the members protested.

"Now, now," the group leader said, "I know that all of you can talk about the Joke all night. But perhaps our newest member is right. Perhaps we should all stop for the evening and get some rest, for the greater glory of the church!''

Everyone seemed to agree with that. There was a round of applause, then all the others followed Dick from the room.

Dick took a deep breath. The coolness of the air in the hall washed over him, bringing him to a point where he felt almost awake. He walked slowly back in the direction Sharon and he had come from, back toward the big hall and the party. He noticed that Sharon kept pace with him on his right side, while the group leader stayed close by his left. The rest of the group walked close behind.

"Well," Dick said slowly, still feeling as if his brain were covered by a layer of cotton, "this has been very—instructive. I'll have to come back soon and talk to you again." And maybe, he thought, next time I'll get on my own and explore rather than get stuck in a never-ending meeting.

"Oh," Sharon said brightly, "you can't leave now."

Dick shook his head. He no longer had any patience for their evangelical enthusiasm. "I'm sorry. I've had a long day."

The group leader put a hand on Dick's shoulder. "I'm sorry, Dick. You don't understand. It's late at night. The church is locked. There's no way to let you out."

Dick stopped and stared at the other man. "The church—is locked?"

The leader nodded solemnly. "Reverend Droll does it every night before he leaves. He does it for our own protection."

Dick was finding this hard to believe. "So you can't get out?"

"No," the leader explained patiently, "so that other people can't get in. You have to understand, Dick, there are a lot of people out there who aren't as open to the church as you are. People who would want to do us harm, or lure us from the warm comfort of the Joke."

"And we don't live in the safest neighborhood," Sharon added. "It's dangerous out there late at night."

They were trapped in here? What if there was a fire? And what had happened to all the people who were here earlier?

"But what about the party?" Dick asked.

Both Sharon and the group leader laughed as if Dick had told a tremendous joke.

"Oh, the party's been over for hours," the leader explained.

"We just get so involved in our little talks," Sharon enthused, "we forget all about the time!"

"Don't worry, Dick," the leader reassured him. "We have plenty of room to sleep."

"Things can look bad late at night, especially when you're tired," Sharon added. "But wait until tomorrow. Everything will look so much brighter!"

She was probably right. Nothing really bad had gone on tonight. It had just gone on for so long. Besides, with his acrobatic training, Dick could always find a way out of this place. He yawned. He could find a way out if he was awake enough to think.

"Come on, Dick," the leader said as he took Dick's arm. "We'll find you a bed in the men's wing."

Sharon waved as Dick was led away. "And remember!"

she called. "The longer you're here, the closer you are to the Joke!"

Dick decided he didn't care about the Joke. He didn't care about anything except sleep.

Bruce Wayne closed his eyes. He was having trouble focusing on the screen. Exhaustion was finally overwhelming him. Through accessing the computers down in the cave below, he found out what he needed to know, and what he had expected.

It had taken him close to an hour of cross-checking police files and records from City Hall, but he knew now that the fish-processing plant was owned by the Joyful Novelty Company. That company, in turn, had been formed by a loose consortium called the Friends for a Happier Gotham City. The Friends shared office space with another organization called the Gotham City Boosters. And the mailing address for the Boosters was the same post office box used by the Church of Perpetual Happiness.

Funny, he thought, that he'd find the connection through a post office box. Perhaps the church—or The Joker— thought that the chain of cover organizations was long enough so that they didn't have to worry about discovery.

Or maybe they specifically structured the chain for the benefit of someone like Batman. Maybe he was supposed to discover this all along. This warehouse could be as much of a trap as that bomb in the half-finished condo. But a trap for whom?

It looked like a trap for Bruce Wayne, at the very least. Apparently the church, or whoever was using the church, wanted to get Bruce Wayne for other than financial reasons.

And maybe there was the beginning of a pattern here,

one shared by the abduction of Winter. Apparently, they liked to lure their victims to locations familiar to someone connected with this church. Even the times of the invitation were similar. Maybe they only took their victims at twilight.

But, this time, that would work against them.

The darker it was, the more it suited Batman.

Bruce shook his head. He had to concentrate on the facts before him. Even if the methods were the same, that left nothing but new questions. What was The Joker's connection? And how did those dead men in the Batman costumes fit in?

Maybe Dick could find some more substantial pattern inside the Church of Perpetual Happiness. He hoped that his former sidekick could find a way to call and keep him informed. Bruce had to admit, if he had known The Joker was involved, he would never have gotten Dick into the middle of it.

The dead body of an adolescent, torn apart by the bomb.

Bruce blinked, and tried to focus his attention back on the screen. Dick couldn't get killed while in a church, could he?

With The Joker, anything was possible.

Unless, of course, Batman got to The Joker first.

Bruce Wayne's head slumped forward. He'd have to stop this and go to bed, any minute now.

Any minute now.

Winter opened his eyes.

There had been no explosion, no bullet.

The Joker pressed the cold muzzle of the revolver against Winter's forehead and pulled the trigger two more times. The hammer clicked on empty cylinders.

"Bang, bang," The Joker said as he pulled the revolver away.

"What are you doing to me?" Winter whispered.

"To whom?" The Joker replied graciously. "You don't exist anymore, do you? As I recall it, you are no longer with us." He stepped back and waved at Dr. Andrews, who now stood beside him. "We do have a new guest, however."

The doctor must have walked in while Winter had his eyes closed. Any small hope Winter had had vanished the instant the doctor arrived. The electrical shocks always started a moment later.

"There is no more Steven Winter," The Joker said.

"I don't see a Steven Winter," the doctor agreed.

"Doctor," The Joker asked, "if you will give him the injection?"

"Gladly." The doctor stepped forward. By now, Winter knew better than to flinch away from the hypodermic needle.

"From this moment forward," the doctor remarked pleasantly as he grabbed Winter's forearm, "you are Batman."

16

"Rise and shine!"

What? Dick Grayson groaned. What time was it? He felt like he hadn't slept at all. There was light coming in from the small windows that ran along the upper third of one of the walls, but that light was faint and tinged with pink, as if it was barely dawn.

He looked at his wrist. He sat up and saw his clothes where he had folded them neatly on the table the night before. It wasn't there, either. His watch was gone.

He swung his feet off the old army cot and looked up at Tom, the group leader from the night before, who seemed to be watching him with some amusement.

"Hey!" Dick complained as he lifted his clothes to make sure there was nothing underneath. "Somebody took my watch!"

"Nobody stole anything, Dick," Tom explained patiently. "We put your watch in our safe box after you fell asleep. We don't want any artificial distractions like time interfering with our business for the church."

Dick had almost had enough of this. "So I can't have my watch?"

"Oh, certainly," Tom replied with far too much good cheer for this hour of the morning. "We'll give it to you when you leave. But while you're participating in church activities, it stays in the box. That's one of the rules around here."

Dick nodded. He had to be careful. He was so tired he might say something he'd regret. He had to act as open as possible until he had a chance to explore the church.

The other men—mostly fellows around Dick's age—who had slept in this huge room were up and walking around, retrieving their clothes from pegs on the walls. Dick guessed there were close to three dozen people in here, with no place for privacy and maybe only a hook on the wall for private possessions.

Besides watches, Dick wondered if there was anything else church members weren't allowed to have. He quietly checked his pants as he pulled them on. The wallet still bulged slightly in the back pocket. So they hadn't taken that. Dick would have to wait until he was alone to check inside his wallet to see if they'd taken anything inside.

He unsuccessfully tried to stifle a yawn. He was so groggy, he didn't know how he could stand.

"So!" Tom called to everybody in the room. "How about some breakfast?"

That sounded good. Dick realized he hadn't eaten anything since yesterday afternoon, hours before he'd come to the church. That could be half of his problem right there. With a good breakfast in him, he should be able to think much more clearly, even shake off this grogginess.

He lined up with the others on one side of the room.

"We have a special treat for you this morning," Tom announced when everyone was in his place. "We ended up making far too much for the party last night. So, this morning we get to eat the leftovers!"

Everybody around Dick cheered as if that was the greatest news they had ever heard. Dick hadn't really gotten a good look at the refreshments from the night before. The spread must be pretty elaborate to get this sort of reaction.

Tom unlocked and opened the door. The others followed him out into the hall, marching single file. As they paraded out of the room, everybody sang a repetitive, four-line song about how happy they were it was morning.

In a funny sort of way, this all reminded Dick of summer camp.

They walked back to the main hall where the party had been held the night before. A women's group, maybe slightly smaller than the men's contingent, waited patiently on the far side of the hall for the males to file in. Sharon smiled and waved at Dick as he stumbled into the room. How could she be so bright and happy this early in the morning? Could she have discovered something in this church's philosophy that actually worked?

Dick looked over at the table, heaped with last night's frosted baked goods, and a pair of clear glass bowls filled with a bright pink liquid. Apparently, they were going to eat these sugary sweets and drink warm punch for breakfast. There wasn't anything else. And this was what everybody was so excited about?

But his mouth was watering, too. Dick had to admit it.

He was famished. Maybe even this food would give him strength.

Tom and a woman at the head of the other line both clapped their hands. "Let's give thanks to Reverend Droll for the food we are about to receive!" the two called together.

"Thank you, Reverend Droll," fifty-odd voices rumbled around Dick.

"And now," Tom continued, "by the great mercy of the Church of Perpetual Happiness, we may eat."

The lines moved in an orderly fashion to the table, as Tom and his female counterpart handed out plates full of gooey sweets. Dick received his in turn, a piece of cake, a couple sugar-glazed cookies, and a cupcake that seemed to be mostly white frosting. He got himself a cup of punch to help wash all this down.

"Looks yummy, doesn't it?" a woman's voice said. He looked up to see Sharon standing by his side. "Let's find a corner where we can talk while we have breakfast."

Dick followed her to the far wall of the church, where they both sat against the wall.

"Let's eat," Sharon said.

Dick took a large bite of fudge cake.

"Wow," Sharon remarked between wolfing down sugar cookies. "They'd never let me eat breakfasts like this at home."

Dick almost laughed. He felt light-headed, the sugar fighting with the exhaustion in his body, so that he felt like he wanted to both run and collapse at the same time.

"So," Sharon asked, "have you thought at all about what we talked about last night?"

"We?" Dick asked. It seemed that the two of them

hadn't had time to talk about much of anything. Had he forgotten something?

"You and me and Tommy and the group," she explained. "You certainly were in the meeting long enough. What's the matter? Not quite awake yet?"

"No, I'm awake," Dick managed. But not awake enough to think, he added to himself. The dry fudge cake seemed to stick in his throat. He took a swig of the warm punch to wash the food down. The liquid was so sweet it almost made him gag.

He was feeling really dizzy. It was hard for him to keep his head up.

He had to get out of here. He'd be no use to himself, or to Batman, if he got himself sick.

"I really have to go." He put his plate down. If he could get over this dizziness, he'd stand up. He tried to take a deep breath.

"Really?" Sharon looked terribly upset, as if Dick had told her someone had died. "I'm sorry to hear that."

"Hey," Dick said after inhaling again. The oxygen did seem to help a little. "I'm not saying I'm not coming back. I really want to learn more about your church. There's just a few things I have to do."

"A few things?" Sharon impulsively grabbed Dick's hands. "Can't they wait? If you go now, you'll miss out on so much."

Dick pulled his hand away as another wave of dizziness overcame him. He couldn't be held down. He had to go. "No, sorry. I have to go. You can't keep me here."

Whoops. The dizziness must be making him paranoid. That last thing he'd said had sounded too negative. He smiled weakly at Sharon. "Sorry," he said again.

"Nobody's keeping you here, Dick," a man's voice said from a few feet away. Dick looked up to see Tom. How long had he been standing there?

"We're all here because we want to be here," Sharon added quickly.

"You don't want to leave just yet," another fellow said as he stepped up next to Tom. "It's Thursday."

Thursday? What was that supposed to mean? Dick groaned and pushed himself into a squat, then, using the wall for support, slowly straightened his knees until he was standing.

"Thursday is the day we get a visit from Reverend Droll," Tom explained.

Reverend Droll? Maybe, Dick thought, he should try to stay around after all. From what Batman had told him, nobody ever got to meet Reverend Droll. If only Dick didn't feel so bad.

"Look," Tom continued, a note of concern in his voice. "Dick's new here. He's not used to our regimens. We can't expect him to keep up with the rest of us just yet." He reached a hand down toward the woman next to Dick. "Sharon? I think Dick needs some fresh air. Why don't you help him out to the courtyard?"

"Sure, Tommy," Sharon agreed brightly. "I'm sorry. Sometimes we might get a little overzealous here in the church. But it's always for a good cause!" She held out her hand. "Here. Let me help you. You've got nothing wrong that a little air and sunshine won't cure!"

Dick took her arm, and she led them back away from the front door. The courtyard must be in the back of the church. He was feeling better just by moving his muscles. He'd just sit in the sun for a few minutes and consider his options without all these people around him. Maybe, if this dizziness passed, he'd stick around and see what he could determine by observing the Reverend Droll. But he'd only do that if he felt much better than he did now. Maybe he'd just get up and go, and come back this evening in time for Droll's appearance. Yes, that made sense. It would give him a chance to get his wits back in working order. So he would simply walk away. If he was outside, there was no way they could stop him.

Sharon stopped and opened a door on the left, a door that looked no different from any of the others that lined the hall.

"Here's our courtyard," she explained as she led him outside, onto a flagstone path into what was probably once a formal rose garden before it was left to grow wild. It was a large space, with the church building stretching off on two sides, and shorter, perhaps ten-foot-high, grey stone walls enclosing the yard.

There was no opening in those walls. From here, Dick couldn't even see a door. He was outside the church building proper, but still surrounded by the church.

There was no way he could get out of here.

Light. Light and a deafening roar. He was too late. He hadn't warned Robin in time. He was too late. Light. Brilliant light.

"Sir?"

Bruce Wayne started awake. He looked up at bright letters on the computer screen, still showing the same file he had called up as he had fallen asleep—how many hours ago?

"Would you care for some breakfast?" Alfred asked.

Bruce stood up and stretched. His muscles were stiff from the way he had slept in the chair.

"Perhaps a little later, Alfred," he replied. He had to get up, take a shower, perhaps work out the kinks in his muscles down in the gym; but most of all he had to think.

He had lost a Robin not long ago. He had lost a friend. And now he had put another friend in jeopardy, perhaps right in the middle of The Joker's newest plot.

And Dick hadn't communicated with Bruce since he'd entered the church. Not a crucial sign—at most, Dick had been in the church half a day. Normally, this would only be a cause for concern if Dick had not reached Bruce or Gordon by the end of the day. But that was before The Joker stepped in.

The Joker could kill anyone, anytime, with no warning. Batman knew that all too well.

There was only one way for Bruce to put his mind at ease. He had to get in touch with Dick as soon as possible and let him know. Every minute was critical as long as Dick was trapped in The Joker's organization.

Bruce decided to give Gordon a call. Maybe the police could arrange a special inspection of some sort, anything to get word in to Dick.

He didn't know what he'd do if he lost a second Robin.

It was on all the time.

Not that he knew what time was anymore. Time blurred. He slept. He woke up. He felt needles in his arm. Someone pushed food between his lips. The video screen was always there, blaring brightly just beyond his cell. And a man said the same three words to him over and over again:

"You are Batman."

He opened his eyes. Batman's image swung across the video screen. The Joker stood on the ground and laughed.

Batman hit The Joker.

Yeah, he could relate to that. Winter so much wanted
to hit—
Winter?
Who was Winter?
Winter was dead.
He was Batman.

17

Commissioner Gordon picked up the phone.

"MacPhee here," the voice of his old friend announced from the other end of the line.

"Graham," Gordon replied to the head of the building and fire codes division of the city government. "How did the surprise inspection go?"

"It didn't, I'm afraid, Jim," MacPhee admitted. "Those bastards at the Church of Perpetual Happiness won't let me in the door without a search warrant."

"Even though you're a city official?" Gordon asked incredulously.

"The only official they recognize is the Reverend Droll," MacPhee stated in an angry singsong that emphasized his Scottish burr. "They are some of the most arrogant sons of bitches I've met in twenty-odd years of building inspection."

"So, what now?" Gordon asked. "Can you get a judicial order?"

"Not this late in the day. I'll do the paperwork right away, Jim, but you know as well as I do it's hard to rush this sort of civil thing. With luck, we should get the paperwork approved to get in there, say, first thing Monday morning."

Damn, Gordon thought. He tried not to let the disappointment show too much in his voice. "I see. Well, I'll see what I can do on this end. Thanks, Graham."

Gordon hung up the phone. He could see MacPhee's problem. It would even be tough for a police commissioner to get a judge to believe that—what? The future of Gotham City was being threatened by a borderline church with a couple hundred members?

Now, if they could somehow come up with something that could tie Winter's disappearance, or The Joker, in with the interior of the church building. He'd have to come up with something.

In the meantime, though, what could he tell Batman?

Sometimes working for somebody else could be a real pain.

Samson had been so disappointed they weren't going to do Gordon. He so wanted to see the expression on that police commissioner's face when he realized he was just another piece of meat that Samson was going to deliver to The Joker for improvement. Yeah, improvement.

"Gordon!" Samson would say. "Remember when you sent me up? Well, I'm back, but you're never coming back. Never!"

But he had to do this Bruce Wayne first. Who was this guy—some sort of sop millionaire? Why did The Joker even bother to pay somebody with Samson's skills to take an easy mark like that?

Samson could always use the money, and this job would be so little sweat that he'd be primed when they did Gordon next. The Joker always had such complete plans for the places Samson was to do his jobs, he knew right where he would snatch him, in the narrow corridor between the fish freezers and the loading dock. Samson did appreciate someone who was prepared.

One more day and this Bruce Wayne would be out of the way, and The Joker could do whatever he wanted with him.

And then Samson got to do Gordon.

Dr. Andrews turned on the lights.

"And what progress are we making, my good doctor?"

The Joker leered up from the chair on the far side of the room. He had been sitting here, alone in the dark. Andrews had promised himself he would not be startled by The Joker's actions. So far, unfortunately, the doctor had not been able to make good on this promise.

"Good, good," Dr. Andrews replied, not really meaning it. If he were being honest, which he seldom was, Dr. Andrews might have said he was doing the best with what he had available.

Working for The Joker did have its disadvantages. Although his employer did seem to have an almost inexhaustible supply of funds, these cramped working conditions still left something to be desired. And, in some cases, the raw materials were so—lacking. Andrews could do nothing but shake his head.

It certainly used to be so much easier when he could work for someone with more stability, especially those dictators and terrorist organizations that operated right out in the open. These political changes of late had made life a bit tedious. Places the doctor had been welcome for years suddenly found him a potential embarrassment. New governments were examining mental hospital records, even prison interrogation techniques! Strong, centralized, no-nonsense dictatorial systems were beginning to break down. Nations all over the globe were actually starting to cooperate. What was going to happen to the world?

Dr. Andrews had decided he shouldn't remain in the political arena long enough to find out. Fortunately, The Joker had been doing a bit of work with some of the doctor's better customers in Iran about that time. And with a minimum of fuss, the new Dr. Andrews had a new country, a new career, and, most important of all, a place to continue his experiments without the meddling of so-called authorities.

"Shall we go see our specimens?" The Joker said.

Of course, Andrews had to agree. He refolded the charts he had carried into the room and put them back in the "Current Projects" cabinet, then followed The Joker on their regular afternoon rounds.

One by one, they checked up on all five of their current residents, each one kept in his own soundproofed cell so that none knew that any of the others existed—indeed, so they only knew that three people existed in the world—the doctor, The Joker, and themselves. Mind control was so much more effective when you controlled the universe of the subject.

"Cell One," The Joker announced as he flipped the switch to remove the shatterproof glass shield that covered the bars.

"And how is our Batman today?"

This time, Subject One didn't answer at all. He sat on a corner of his cot, staring at the wall.

"Hey, batboy!" The Joker crooned. "It's your old friend. Can't you take a joke?"

There was no response.

"This is going to take some personal attention." The Joker pressed a second button. The cell door swung open. The Joker strolled jauntily across the room to the figure in the cowl and cape.

"Hey!" He grabbed the man in grey and turned him to face him. "It's The Joker! Nyah, nyah, nyah! Remember me?"

The Batman stared past The Joker as if he didn't even see the other man.

"The Joker!" Andrews's employer insisted. "You know, the guy who killed your little Robin? Come on, how about a nice hello?"

Batman twisted his head away to look back at the same spot on the wall.

"He has been in here too long," the doctor fretted. "We cannot have them here for weeks on end. They need to have some outside stimulation for the programming to take hold."

"Actually," The Joker admitted, "there's something in me that likes my Batman this way. But I see what you mean. This guy would be no fun at all at parties." He turned and strolled out of the cell to rejoin the doctor. "Shall we proceed?"

The doctor grunted and they walked across the corridor to Subject Three. The Joker pressed the button to remove the glass.

"Scum!" Batman screamed. He ran forward, smashing his fists against the bars. "I'll kill both of you! I'll smash you! I'll cut you into little pieces and eat them raw! I'll—''

The Joker closed the glass. ''No problem here.''

The doctor wasn't so sure. Each of these batmen seemed to be unraveling in his own way. These were the early experiments, before Andrews had had a chance to fine-tune his programs, before he had determined what it really meant to be someone like Batman. He had, of course, fed them all the supplementary tapes as he had developed them, but their character foundations were not quite as strong as his more recent projects. The doctor had considered stripping away their rebuilt personalities and starting over again—that, in itself, could be a fascinating experiment—but The Joker kept him busy with so much fresh material, any such personality revision would have to wait.

''Number Four,'' The Joker announced as they reached the next cell, the one that contained the subject that worried the doctor the most. The Joker rolled away the glass.

''Keep away!'' the man inside screamed. ''I'm Batman!''

''Not much change here either, I see,'' The Joker mused. ''Perhaps if I added some sensory input.'' He pressed the second button, and the cell door opened.

''Keep away!'' the man inside called, softer than before. His tone was more pleading than belligerent. ''Keep away. You know who I am.''

The Joker stepped inside the cell. ''And you know who I am.''

''Yeah,'' the man in the Batman costume replied. ''I know, I know. And I want you to go.''

The Joker stopped midstride, looking even more delighted than usual. ''Wait a second! Did I detect a rhyme?''

The other man nodded. "Have no fear. Batman's here."

"What a wonderful development!" The Joker cheered. He abruptly made an about-face and marched out of the cell. "This is one line of thought we definitely want to encourage." He closed the cell door behind him and patted the doctor on the shoulder. "You know, this is a Batman we definitely *could* take to parties!"

The doctor wished he could be as sure of all this as his employer. "Their egos are too unstable. They need some outside reinforcement. They need some action."

"Hey, Doc, we *all* need some action. Grown men, and we spend all our time in a cell block!" He shook his head. "Maybe I should let them out all at once! A world full of bumbling batmen!" The Joker roared.

Sometimes, Dr. Andrews wondered if his employer took all of this seriously. He would never know. There were some questions you simply didn't ask your superiors.

The Joker stopped laughing as abruptly as he had begun. "Shall we visit our star pupils?"

The doctor followed as The Joker danced down the corridor to Subject Six—their latest, finest Batman.

"God damn it, Joker!" the sixth Batman raged as he pulled to the limits of his restraints. He looked quite good in the new costume, too. He had good muscle tone, and the "Batman" seamstresses were getting better.

"You're laughing now," "Batman" shouted as he shook his fist, "but I'll get you soon enough!"

"Perfect!" The Joker chuckled. "He even sounds like Batman—no sense of humor at all!" He patted Andrews on the back. "Doctor, you get better and better."

"I do my best," Andrews replied humbly as he glanced at the chart outside the cell. "I believe it is time for another injection."

The new "Batman"'s bravado was gone, replaced by a look of panic. "No, you can't! You can't do that to Batman!"

"My dear fellow," The Joker replied. "We can do whatever we want to Batman, anytime we want to. Now, why not be a good Batman and show us that arm?"

Batman listened to the dial tone for a moment before he hung up the phone. He didn't like the sound of this. This could be very bad for Dick.

Gordon had called him and told him how they couldn't legally enter the headquarters of the Church of Perpetual Happiness. The commissioner had explained how the church members were within their legal rights, and how difficult it was to get a search warrant against a church.

Batman thought again about the paper flowers and the deck of cards. It was one of the ways The Joker taunted him, by leaving these clues at the scene of a crime. The Joker always seemed driven to tip his hand to show his involvement, as if his caper wasn't complete without Batman's knowledge.

According to the information Gordon had given Batman, this church was amassing great amounts of unreported, and untraceable, cash—far more than The Joker could gather in a dozen of his elaborate robberies. If The Joker really was running this church, all he had to do was keep quiet and he would be both rich and beyond the control of the law. He had no need to either stage those robberies, or to let anybody know he had anything to do with the church.

But The Joker was not a sane man. Maybe he wanted to be caught. Maybe he wanted to challenge the Batman. Maybe his crimes were never complete unless the Batman was involved. That last reason would certainly explain why these men in Batman costumes had been found at crime scenes. If The Joker needed a Batman, now he could produce them at his convenience, and kill them off at his convenience as well.

Crimes were sweeter for The Joker when Batman was involved. He had sworn that he could no longer treat the Joker as an obsession. That would result in the destruction of them both. But Batman found The Joker's latest scheme too personal. Dick was in that church, and for all Batman knew, The Joker was in there, too.

And then Gordon had told him the police were unable to search the church. Sometimes lawbreakers could twist the law so it protected the guilty.

But that was one of the reasons he had become Batman. Unlike Gordon, Batman did not always have to rigidly observe written codes and legal niceties. He could take one step beyond the law, and confront evil at its darkest heart.

Dick was out there, and he couldn't lose him, not like he'd lost Jason. No matter what problems Grayson and he had had these past days, even these past years, they were like family, closer than father and son, more like brothers, in the way they fought together, the way they understood each other.

He'd lashed out against Dick for things he hadn't liked in himself. Dick was so close to him that he could make him feel—and he didn't dare feel, not after the way Jason had died. The realization hit him harder than any blow he'd ever taken from a fist.

It also made him admit how much he had needed Dick around, how he had needed the conversation, the camaraderie, even the reflection of himself in a younger person.

Any man, even a man who tried to be as strong as Batman, could not exist completely alone. It was this relationship, this feeling, he had tried, unsuccessfully, to reproduce when he had taken on another apprentice crime fighter, a new Robin.

Jason.

The Joker had shown himself again, and now Batman knew what he had to do. He would avenge Jason's death, and save Dick from The Joker's plans. The Joker needed to keep Batman close, to inform Batman of his plans. This time, Batman would use The Joker's needs to destroy his nearest foe.

But Batman could not let his own emotion overcome him. There could be no way for The Joker to know he had the former Robin under his control. Dick was trained to protect himself. He might be held prisoner, but there was no reason to think he had come to any great harm.

Batman's logic said all these things, but the emotions, that part of Batman that was almost always hidden, said something else.

If there was no change by nightfall, Batman would open the church by himself.

18

Dick woke with a start.

"There he is!" someone called.

"I knew he'd wake up in time," another voice added.

"Dick, you're going to make a great addition to the church!"

Dick couldn't remember falling asleep. Actually, he couldn't remember much specific about most of this day. He and Sharon had come out here to the courtyard early in the morning, and had been joined a minute later by some more members of the church. People had started to talk, and Dick had done his best to listen. He had felt trapped for a moment, but had decided it was best not to panic. If he had to stick around here all day, he might as well learn what he could, and then see what he could find out about Reverend Droll this evening. After that, he'd see about leaving; peacefully, if possible.

More people had joined them as the sun had risen above the courtyard. Everybody had been talking, and Dick had found himself talking, too. Some of these other church members made sense talking about relationships. Dick had been too uptight about the people around him—Batman, Kory, the Titans—he had to let these things go. The Church of Perpetual Happiness was good at helping you let things go.

Somewhere in there, they ate again, fast food from some local takeout joint, not great, but better than breakfast. More than once in there, he'd fallen asleep, too, probably because of the late hour he'd been up to the night before.

But when he was awake, everything around him was starting to make sense. Somehow, he knew the Joke would make him happy.

He looked up and saw Sharon's smiling face. "I'm glad you woke up. You've been a little under the weather."

Under the weather? Was that why he'd been sleeping so much?

"But it's almost time!" she added. Her face, caught in the last glow of the sun as it slipped beneath the wall, seemed to shine with excitement.

"Time?" he asked. His voice was hoarse, his throat dry.

"For Reverend Droll," she explained.

It was Thursday night already? He must have slept longer than he had thought.

"I envy you," one of the men said as he looked over Sharon's shoulder. Dick knew him. It was Larry, from the day before. "You will have the privilege of meeting Reverend Droll for the first time. Oh, Dick, I wish I could have that experience all over again! Your mind is as asleep in its way as if you were still napping in the sun. But when you meet Droll, he will wake you up!''

"Yes!" the others yelled. "Yes! Wake up! Wake up!"

"The Reverend Droll makes everybody feel better," Sharon agreed. "That's part of the power of the Joke."

"Let's go wait for the reverend!" Larry called. Everyone stood up, and Dick was lifted up along with them. He found himself in the middle of a mass of moving bodies. When his feet hit the ground, he walked. When he was a little slow, he was carried, with the rest of them, as the whole congregation returned to the church. They all sang a simple song about how good it was to wake up. It was a very happy song.

If Dick's throat hadn't been so dry, his voice so hoarse, he would have sung along.

The Joker had to admit it: This was as much fun as one guy could have without killing people. To think, instead of destroying, he was creating—Batman after Batman! Each one was different, and every one was crazy in his own very individual way.

But it got better still at the end. After he and the doctor were done with the batmen, they had to see to their very special project, the one closest to The Joker's big, open, continually bleeding heart. It was time to visit the man who, in his pitifully inadequate former existence, had been known as Big Mike, remade now in the only image that really mattered—that of The Joker!

The real, actual, accept-no-substitutes Joker chuckled as Dr. Andrews led the way. The poor doctor. He was only in this for the money, and maybe something stupid like scientific curiosity.

The Joker was in this for love.

For love of Batman, first, for how could The Joker exist without his Batman? How boring life would be without a worthy nemesis! The Joker and Batman were much more than good guy vs. bad guy. They were night and day, crime and punishment, trickster and straight man, and oh, so much more!

The Joker was sometimes a little hurt that Batman didn't appreciate him more. That was, of course, one of the main reasons he'd killed the second Robin—to get that Bat guy's attention! And if you couldn't get Batman to appreciate you, why not make a few of your own that you'd make sure knew who the real super-villain was around here!

And then, once he'd built his better batmen, he'd send them out on specially developed robberies. If they succeeded in defeating the robbers, he'd know he had a batman worth keeping. And if the robbers killed the "Batman" instead, what the hey, The Joker got all that money! As far as he could see, this was a real win-win situation.

And it got better! Once The Joker got a working "Batman" of his very own, what was to keep him from killing the real thing? Hey who would know the difference especially when you're talking about somebody as wooden as Batman?

After he'd killed the boring old bat, of course, he'd always keep one or two of the substitutes around, you know, to swing down from tall buildings, accept civic awards, maybe even foil the occasional crime The Joker would specially set up for the occasion. The Joker's very own batboys—they'd give him all the thrills without the risks.

This was so good, he didn't know how he could top it. Well, maybe he could start with this guy in the cell here.

What a handsome face he had, with that delicate chalk-white pallor, those temptingly wide, bloodred lips—and wherever could you see the likes of his lustrous, bright green hair? (Only his hairdresser knew for sure!)

The Joker laughed as he pushed the button to remove the glass.

The man who had been Big Mike tried to laugh back. It came out more like a gargled groan.

The Joker was appalled. "He can't laugh! Why can't he laugh?"

"He's in too much pain," the doctor explained. "The surgical scars on his face, where we restructured his lips and cheekbones—they've barely begun to heal."

Oh, dear. This was upsetting. The Joker didn't like it when things got upsetting. "Barely begun to heal? I don't have that kind of time! We come up with a wonderful new technique that changes a man's brain in a matter of days, and you tell me we have to wait for weeks for the face to follow?"

Dr. Andrews took a step away, as if he half expected The Joker to lash out. Dr. Andrews knew The Joker pretty well.

"I'm afraid so," the doctor answered quietly. "I alter the human brain by using the fears and doubts that already exist inside it, building my changes on the foundations of my subject's neuroses. The plastic surgery, though perhaps less complex scientifically, is in its way a more wholesale change and requires the comparatively slow healing process of the human body."

"So you say," The Joker replied brusquely. "I will have to speak to my team of surgeons concerning alternatives. In the meantime, what will we do here with Mr.

Pain?'' He pressed the first button again, and the glass shield slid back down the bars. He turned to the doctor.

"Maybe we will have to use our first Joker for something special.''

The sun was gone, and there was still no word from Gordon.

Batman had climbed into his car at sunset, and was already on his way. Part of him thought that perhaps it would be better if he waited until later, when the church members would be asleep. But the other, deeper part of him knew he had to act now.

The Batmobile glided silently through the outskirts of the city, past late commuters and couples going to early parties. Sometimes this was Bruce Wayne's world, full of day-to-day tasks and social obligations. Tonight, it seemed like a foreign place to the Batman. He had only two reasons for being. He had to save Dick Grayson. And he had to make sure The Joker never hurt anybody ever again.

Before he had left, he had used his computer to call up his detailed maps for the quarter of the city that held the Church of Perpetual Happiness. It was one of the oldest areas of Gotham, full of warehouses and tenements, although much of the overcrowded, substandard housing had been burned out, leaving empty, rubble-strewn lots that went on for blocks.

The church itself was on a large, still-wooded lot, a phenomenally expensive piece of real estate, even in that corner of town. But the lot gave him an excellent place to hide the Batmobile, and an unobtrusive way to examine the church before he made his move.

Batman pulled his car off the river highway and drove

two of the three blocks to the church before taking a cross street that led to the walled, wooded lot. This outer wall was in as bad repair as the surrounding neighborhood. It wouldn't keep anybody out, but it offered plenty of places to hide. There had once been an iron gate that covered the entrance to the fire road Batman wanted to use, but only one half of the wrought iron was left, propped against the remaining brickwork. Batman drove straight in through the weeds, already high for so early in spring.

He saw a few figures running as he drove beyond the gate. Dealers and junkies, most likely—this overgrown lot seemed to be the perfect place to conduct that kind of business. Maybe, after he and the police had cleaned up the church, Batman would come back here and do some more cleaning of his own.

He left the Batmobile underneath a copse of trees. Almost as an afterthought, he activated a device that would send a small electrical shock through anyone who touched the vehicle. In a place like this, it was probably wise to discourage the curious. Not that anyone with any sense would fool with something like the Batmobile. Sometimes, though, Batman ran into people with no sense left at all.

He cut through the trees to his left. According to his calculations, the church should be about three hundred yards ahead.

"I'd stop where you were," a voice called out from the undergrowth.

Batman paused. It was dark. He had made very little noise. Had someone been waiting for him?

A bright light shone in his face. Then another.

A number of voices spoke in low tones ahead. One said something about "hearing the alarm." There were half a dozen lights around him now, all powerful flashlight beams.

"You are trespassing on church property," the same voice said.

Batman wasn't going to be stopped now. He took a step forward. The beams all shifted with him.

"We are within our rights to use force," the voice went on without emotion.

"I am in pursuit of a known felon," Batman replied, disguising the truth very slightly. "My information indicates he could be hiding on these grounds."

"Impossible," the voice replied. "We know everyone who comes through here. You have ten seconds to turn around, thirty to reach your vehicle, a minute to leave church grounds."

Batman turned. There were too many of them to fight effectively. They had the advantage for now.

"I wouldn't come back here, either!" the voice called after him. "The Church of Perpetual Happiness doesn't like your kind!"

Batman didn't bother to reply. He knew for certain that he would be back here again.

19

All the members of the church whispered excitedly with
one another, like schoolchildren waiting for Santa Claus.
They had gathered in what Dick guessed was the main hall
of worship. Multicolored saints stared down at them from
stained-glass windows, although there were no crosses or
other religious symbols left in the room. All of the pews
had been removed, too, so that all of them had to stand.
A makeshift podium with a microphone had been set up
on the altar.

"Believers!" someone yelled from the back of the room.

Everyone was instantly silent.

"The Reverend Droll is among us!"

It startled Dick when everybody started to laugh. But
laugh they did, and applaud. The din rose to a roar as a
door behind the podium opened and a tall man in crimson
robes emerged. Dick recognized the newcomer from the

videotape Gordon had shown him. It was the Reverend Droll.

Gordon and the videotape; somehow that seemed to have happened very long ago. Dick had to remember he was here to do more than just listen to Reverend Droll. He was here to question things, to see how the church operated.

Reverend Droll grabbed the microphone.

"Friends!" he called to his congregation. "Tell me! Have any of you been truly happy?"

"*Yes!*" came back the deafening reply. Dick was amazed by the fervor of all of those around him. It was incredible to see this many people so full of faith. Maybe they had been right when they talked to him before. Maybe this was the thing that Dick had been missing. He still wished he had been able to find out more about the fundamentals of this church. But maybe now, with the Reverend Droll here, everything would become clear.

"And how is my favorite congregation?" Droll called.

"*Happy!*" was the booming response.

Dick looked up and realized that the reverend was smiling directly at him.

"I understand we have a new face among us tonight."

"Dick," he found himself replying. "Dick—uh—Dick Brown."

Droll reached his hands out toward Dick over the podium. "You are welcome among us, Dick Brown, for we know the pain you have suffered."

The pain he had suffered? Dick frowned. He guessed that was just the way they greeted visitors to their congregation.

"For who among us has not known pain?" Droll called.

"*Yes!*" the congregation called back.

"Who among us has not known misery?"

"Yes!"

"Who among us has not suffered before they found the church?"

"Yes! Yes!" Some of the congregation started to pound their feet on the old wooden floor, setting up a *boom! boom! boom*! rhythm that filled the hall for a minute or more. The Reverend Droll smiled on benignly until they were done.

Droll pointed again. "Dick Brown, you are new among us! But all of us know of your suffering!"

"Yes, Dick!" Individuals shouted around him. "We know!" "We all have suffered!" "We understand!"

"Your surrogate father rejected you!" Droll rumbled. "Your girlfriend left you!"

Dick frowned. How could Droll know all that? Could he really be the divine messenger the church members claimed he was?

"You have no friends in this world except for the church!" Droll exclaimed.

Sharon was hugging him. The church? It was true. The church had accepted him right away. Still, there were an awful lot of questions he'd like to have answered. If only he could remember what they were. People were pounding on the floor again. *Boom! Boom! Boom!*

"Accept the church, Dick!"

"Yes!" all around him screamed.

"Accept us as your friends!"

"Yes! Accept us!"

They wanted to let him in? To be a part of all this happiness? What would it hurt to agree?

Droll raised both his hands to the heavens. "Accept us, be a part of us!"

This joy was infectious. Dick found he really did want to be a part of this.

"*Yes!*" the crowd shouted. "*Yes!*"

"Accept us"—both Droll's hands closed into fists— "and we will all share the Joke!"

"*The Joke!*" the crowd chorused. "*Yes! Yes!*"

The Joke? That was what he was here to find. He had to do it.

Dick smiled and nodded.

"Yes," he said.

"*Yes! Yes! Yes! Yes!*" the crowd and Droll chanted together.

Dick found himself surrounded by arms and hands, patting him, hugging him, lifting him from the ground. He was above a sea of smiling faces, many of them with tears running down their cheeks. He felt overwhelmed.

"In a moment—" Droll called out, and the crowd's noise evaporated at the sound of his voice. "In a moment we will go and induct our newest member into the mysteries. We shall teach him the first level of the Joke!" He paused, his voice shifting to a lower, more serious register. "And as we do so, I want each and every one of you to reflect on what the church has meant to your lives. For the Church of Perpetual Happiness is facing treachery!"

The spirit of joy in the room seemed to freeze. It was as if the sun had vanished completely from the sky in the middle of the Fourth of July. The change was that abrupt. Dick found he missed the spontaneous joy.

"There are those who would compromise us," Droll continued quickly. "Those we have thought of as friends, but are scheming to undermine us. All of us might have to fight for the greater glory of the Joke!"

"*Yes!*" the crowd shouted. "*Yes!*"

And as quickly as that, the joy was back.

"Come now!" Droll exhorted the others. "Let's bring Dick Brown into the fold. It is time for the Joke!"

The following roar cut off abruptly, interrupted by a heavy pounding on the church's great double doors.

"Open up!" an amplified voice came through the wood. "Police!"

Gordon had finally gotten the go-ahead.

It felt like he'd had to spend the past six hours trying to call in every favor with every member of the judicial system he'd ever spoken with in his entire career. Even his old buddy Judge Garman didn't want to disturb a church—the whole separation of church and state again —until Gordon had shown him the videotape of their questionable solicitation practices. It might not have gotten him any convictions, but it did get him a search warrant. And this time there was no reason Gordon couldn't go himself.

He gathered a dozen of his best men. Unfortunately, he couldn't reach Batman. He decided to leave him a message and move on. It had taken so long to get the authorization, he didn't want to wait any longer. He was sure Batman would understand, even approve. They had to open up that church and find a young man answering to the name of Dick Brown before anything more could happen to him.

Fifteen minutes later, Gordon stood with a bullhorn, making demands at a still-closed double door.

"Police!" he called again. "We've got a warrant."

There was a heavy clank on the other side of the doors. A moment later one of the doors opened.

"The church," a tall, gangly man began, "doesn't believe in worldly things like—"

Gordon didn't even let the man finish. "Push the door in!" he called to the two men closest to him. The officers quickly climbed the steps and pushed the tall man out of the way. Gordon strode in after them.

Gordon could hardly believe what happened next. It was like one of those protests back in the sixties. There must have been close to three hundred people in this room, and every single one of them sat down, side by side, to block any farther progress into the building.

No one moved, except in the back, where a small crowd seemed to be hustling someone, or something, away.

"Commissioner!" Detective Haley yelled as he pointed at one of the young men in the front of the crowd. "Look over here!"

"Oh, my God," Gordon whispered. It was Thompson, the young police officer who had disappeared in the church.

"Thompson!" he called as he rushed over to the man. "Don't you know me? It's Gordon!"

The former rookie cringed as if Gordon were going to hit him. "I don't care how you know my name!" Thompson screamed up at him. "The Joke will protect me!"

Gordon stopped abruptly. What in heaven's name was going on here?

"What is the meaning of this?" a deep voice called from the back of the hall. Gordon looked across the sit-in to see Reverend Droll, dressed in long red robes.

"Reverend Droll," he said evenly, trying not to show the anger that threatened to overwhelm him. "I have a warrant. We will search the building. If you don't cooperate, I'll have you all arrested."

"This sounds like police harassment," Droll replied. "It won't look very good in the papers."

"Will it look any better that you had a disagreement

with the authorities?'' Gordon replied. ''Authorities whom you refused to cooperate with.''

Droll paused for a moment, as if considering his options. He smiled at Gordon. ''Now, now,'' he said in a quieter tone. ''I'm sure there's a way we can work this all out. We can all be reasonable. There's nothing here to hide. We're a charitable organization, after all. I'll personally take you on a tour of the facilities.''

Why this sudden turnaround? Somehow, Gordon felt, they had already missed their chance. Dick Brown, or anybody else being held against their will, would be nowhere to be found.

Still, he had to look. He stepped forward, and Droll's congregation parted before him like the Red Sea.

When Batman got back into the Batmobile, he found a message waiting for him. As soon as he was beyond the church walls, he played it back, and discovered that by now Gordon would have entered the church from the other side.

He drove around to the front of the church, where he found Gordon's car and three police cruisers. All the cars were empty, the street was deserted. He climbed from the Batmobile and hurried up the church steps.

The front doors were closed. Batman knocked. There was no response. He pushed at the door, but apparently they had locked it after the police had gone inside. Strange. The doors were too sturdy to force, unless he ran into them with the front of the Batmobile.

Perhaps, Batman thought, that solution was a little extreme, at least for the moment. He should be patient and wait for a sign of the police. He stepped back from the steps to see if he could spot any other activity around the church, but everything was quiet.

The front door burst open a moment later.

"Please forgive me for my earlier reticence, Commissioner," someone was saying. Batman realized it was Reverend Droll. "Feel free to come back anytime. I think the church and the police can learn to work together."

Gordon didn't say anything as he stormed down the steps. Twelve police officers and plainclothes detectives followed him from the church. There was no one else with them.

The door slammed shut behind them.

"Batman!" Gordon called when he saw him. "You missed quite a show. Though I doubt you could have done any more than we did."

"There was no sign of Nightwing?" Batman asked.

"No. They stopped us from getting through to the interior of the church for close to five minutes, and then gave us a very closely guided tour. Of course, we didn't find a thing. There must be some hidden areas inside the church somewhere—rooms blocked off, that sort of thing. I think your friend is still in there. But it won't do us any good unless we know where to look."

Where to look? Of course.

"Commissioner," Batman stated flatly. "The original blueprints for this church are on file with the building commission."

Gordon nodded. "Along with the plans of any major renovations. Oh, I see what you're getting at."

"We have to find those hidden places before they can move their hostage to another one of their buildings. Can we get in to the commission's offices at this hour?"

"Hell, when you're the police commissioner, you can get in anywhere." He glanced back over his shoulder. "Well, almost anywhere. Let's go take a look, though I don't know how in the world I'm going to get another search warrant to come back here. God, I'd like to find something and put Droll away for a long, long time."

Gordon told a couple of his men to stake out the front of the church and report any unusual activity. The rest of them returned to their cars.

Batman followed the commissioner back to City Hall. One way or another, he would find a way to turn that church inside out.

20

Dick only got the slightest glimpse of the newcomers before he was rushed from the room. But he saw who they were; he saw flashes of blue through the milling congregation.

"You have to get out of here," the voices told Dick. "They are enemies of the reverend." "You can't believe their lies."

But Dick had seen the uniforms of the people who had run into the room, the people he was being protected from. They were policemen. Were these the people Reverend Droll was warning his congregation about—the police? Dick thought he glimpsed Commissioner Gordon as he was hustled from the hall. If Gordon was there, Batman probably was, too.

They were hiding from policemen. They were hiding

from the people Dick had worked with for years, and people who were Dick's friends!

He was rushed down a hallway he had never seen before. What he thought was a panel opened before him. Dick realized it was a doorway. He was pushed into the room and told they would fetch him in a minute. Then the door slammed shut, and he was left in the darkness.

Something else had happened, too. Maybe it was the adrenaline from being hurried from the room like that, maybe it was because he was left alone here, but for whatever reason, Dick felt he was thinking more clearly than he had in a long while.

For the first time since he'd gotten here, he was away from the others and their constant droning voices. Someone was always talking to him, touching him, never giving him a moment to himself. He thought of that constant conversation, and realized, in a way, it could almost be a form of hypnosis, like listening to some soft mantra chanted over and over again. And the talk never ended, even when he was asleep. He had been skeptical at first, but later—what did his subconscious mind get from this talk? Maybe that was why he was so willing to accept all of this.

There may have been other things besides the talk. At the very least, the food wasn't very good. They seemed to pick the stuff with the least nutrition possible. What if they had put something into the food to make him even more susceptible? Here he was, a seasoned crime fighter, who had battled some of the greatest villains Gotham City had ever seen, and here this church had gotten him one step away from selling flowers on street corners!

He couldn't fall under their spell again. He wouldn't

eat anything else, nor would he fall asleep, until he was out of here.

There was a soft knock on the door. Before Dick could say anything, the door opened, and Sharon came into the room carrying an oil-burning lantern. The new light gave Dick a chance to look around. From the ragged-edged molding that stopped just before the doorway Sharon now closed behind her, it looked like the door was part of a false wall, and that this whole space was once part of the larger room beyond.

"We have to stay quiet in here for a while," Sharon said in a whisper. "The Reverend Droll will try to keep the forces of evil completely away from this part of the church, but those who would destroy us have many devious ways. We have to be careful."

It sounded like the woman was reading from some terribly melodramatic book or something. It certainly didn't sound like regular conversation. Yet Dick wouldn't be at all surprised if she was repeating, word for word, what she had been told by one of Droll's assistants. Only a few minutes ago he had been ready to believe things about the church that were nearly as foolish-sounding.

Sharon put down the lantern and stepped close to Dick.

"I have special news," she said. "We've gotten special permission from the reverend. We can stay here together, tonight, all night, all alone." Dick realized there was a certain awe in her voice. "You must be so special to him. You don't know what a privilege this is."

She looked up at him. Even though her face was mostly in shadow, Dick knew she was waiting for him to kiss her. So now the church was going to use sex to keep him quiet?

He remembered how when he had first come here the other night, he had found Sharon attractive, and had even, vaguely, considered that something might happen between them. But he knew now that those feelings had been fueled mostly by what had happened to him before he stepped inside the church, by the way he had felt rejected by his girlfriend. If she didn't want him anymore, he'd find someone else. The church had used those feelings of rejection, both from Starfire and from Bruce, to draw Dick into their web. But while his feelings might be real, the church members twisted them to their own ends; ends Dick no longer wanted to be a part of.

He saw this whole church now as some sort of vicious cycle, with members brainwashing newer members, who in turn would use the same process on newer people. And then what? Raising money for the Joke, whatever that was? Or did the church also put its members to other, not so public uses? Dick decided he wasn't going to stick around to find out. They almost had him under their spell once. He didn't want to risk getting any deeper.

Sharon was still waiting. He didn't want to hurt her. She was no doubt as much a victim as he had been about to become. He put his arms around her. As she hugged him in turn, he found the proper pressure point in her neck and squeezed. She slumped against him, unconscious. He placed her gently on the floor, then went to the door.

At first, there didn't appear to be any way to get the panel open from this side. The door pushed inward, and there was no knob or other handhold to bring the panel in toward him. But if this place was that secure a prison, why had they sent someone to keep him occupied? No, there had to be a way out of here. He felt along the molding below the door and found a place where a groove had been cut.

He brought the lantern over for a closer look. Yes, there was a two-inch piece of molding that looked as if it had been cut away, then replaced. The wood didn't give when Dick pressed it. He tried pushing it up toward the door. The molding shifted, and the door popped open a quarter of an inch. He must have activated a hidden spring. Whatever it was, it gave him a way out of here.

The hall outside his hiding place was every bit as dark as the room had been behind him. It was quiet, too. There didn't seem to be anybody in this part of the church building. Dick considered taking the lantern with him, but decided against it. An unfamiliar light might cause somebody to investigate. He should be able to retrace his steps to the chapel. From there, he'd go out one of the doors or windows.

He stepped out into the hall and felt his way along the wall. He heard voices now, in another part of the church, back, he guessed, toward the men's dormitory room. He had no idea how long he had been in hiding. The police must be gone by now, and the church members herded back to their quarters. Hopefully, that meant there was less chance of being discovered. He didn't know how long his strength would last if he had to fight his way out.

There was a faint light ahead of him. He walked a little faster, careful to move as silently as he could. He passed the corridor that led to the men's wing, and then stepped out into the now-empty chapel.

The light he had seen was from the streetlights outside, filtered into blues and reds by the stained-glass windows. It gave him more than enough illumination to see his way around. There were heavy chains and locks on both the main doors and the side door that Winter had run through—was it only the night before? Dick felt like he had been in this building forever. That meant he had to go through one of the windows.

It was an old wooden podium that looked like it had been picked up secondhand, scraped up but solidly built, probably of maple. Even more important, it wasn't nailed down. He grunted. It was too solidly built for him to lift in his current condition, so he tilted the podium back and forth, using his weight to counterbalance the mass of wood, and walked it forward, first moving one side a foot or so ahead, then the other, until he had lowered the massive block from the altar and pushed it across the room.

He had to pause for a moment, out of breath. He heard a burst of static, and a voice saying, "Checkpoint Three, all okay." It sounded like some sort of night watchman, and Dick imagined he had to be headed right for him.

He pushed the podium under the nearest window, then climbed up to the piece's slanted top. It put him face-to-face with one of the stained-glass saints. He could also see what bad repair the window was in. There were cracks in both the pieces of glass and the leading that held the window together. This close, it looked like the whole thing was about to fall apart. Lucky for him, he guessed. It wouldn't take much of a blow to push the thing out.

Dick quickly pulled off his shirt and wrapped it around his right hand and arm to protect himself as much as possible from being cut by the broken glass.

"Sorry, saint," he whispered.

He smashed the glass, clearing the remaining shards away with his cloth-covered arm. Somebody yelled behind him, but he was already through the window and out on the street. He ducked down an alley across the way and was out of sight of the church before anyone could unlock and open the front door.

He stopped a couple blocks away when he heard no sounds of pursuit. The church was so efficiently designed to keep people in, they probably had never considered that somebody could escape.

Now what could he do? His hopes sank as he checked his pockets.

Sometime, when he slept in the courtyard, the other church members must have decided he was staying. Someone had taken his wallet. His keys were gone, too.

Very well. He only knew of one safe place.

Somehow, he would get there.

21

Alfred threw on his robe and descended the stairs. The first red-gold light of dawn brightened the drawing room below. Who could be at the door at this hour? He had not heard Mr. Wayne come in during the night. Could this have to do with him?

He frowned as he looked through the small window in the front door. It took him a moment to recognize the disheveled person on the other side. But it had to be.

"Alfred." The other man staggered forward as the butler opened the door.

"Master Dick!" Alfred replied.

The young man attempted to nod, but fell at Alfred's feet instead. He had no shirt, and his upper body was covered by dirt and a couple of hearty scratches. He seemed to have passed out on the doorstep.

"Oh, dear," Alfred said softly. Well, he'd best get Dick

inside to someplace warm and comfortable, and see that none of his wounds was too serious.

Alfred sighed. He had years of experience at this sort of thing.

The answer wasn't here.

Piles of paper littered the floor of the commissioner's outer office, while dusty file folders formed great mounds atop every desk, table, file cabinet, even the water cooler. Gordon and he had spent the last four hours poring over not only building records, but every piece of paper relating to the Church of Perpetual Happiness that they could find in all of City Hall. There didn't seem to have been any construction at all in or around that particular church building in the last twenty years. And that building, and the seven other properties that the church owned around town, seemed to be scrupulously legal in terms of fire codes, occupancy rates, elevator inspections, and anything else the city had its hand in, without any sign of chicanery by The Joker, Reverend Droll, or anybody else.

Gordon slammed a file case in frustration. "This is all *too* clean!"

"I don't think I'd say that," a woman's voice said from the doorway.

Both Gordon and Batman turned around.

"Why, Ms. Davis!" the commissioner mumbled apologetically. "Is it that late?"

"Actually, it's quite early," Ms. Davis replied as she checked her watch. "Your new workday isn't supposed to begin for—say—twenty minutes."

Gordon found a chair and sat down with a groan. "I'm sorry. Look what I did to your office!"

"I'm glad you're the one saying that," Ms. Davis replied with a smile. "I hope, at the very least, you found what you were looking for."

Batman and Gordon looked at each other.

"We didn't find anything," Batman admitted.

"Except hours of filing," Ms. Davis replied dryly.

"Oh, dear," Gordon said. "Maybe I'd better put some of this back myself."

"You'll do no such thing," his executive secretary ordered. "And neither will I. An organizational effort of this magnitude calls for some very special talents of, say, a certain assistant commissioner?"

"She's actually putting O'Neal to work?" Batman asked.

"She's the only one who can," Gordon admitted. "An amazing woman. Well, I'd better go down to the men's room and clean myself up for the new day."

"You're not going to do that either," Ms. Davis remarked sternly. "I will be forced to tell all callers that both Commissioner Gordon and Batman have been called away to an emergency, one that should give them at least a few hours of sleep."

"Well," Gordon said slowly, his exhaustion adding to his uncertainty. "If you think so, Ms. Davis."

"It's a fact of life," she replied. "There's nothing I can do about it." She shrugged off her coat and hung it on a hook inside the door. "Now get out of here."

Both men knew when it was best to obey orders.

The Joker was not pleased.

"You are never to come here," he said. "I thought I made that plain."

"You've made more than that very plain," the Reverend Droll insisted. "My organization gives you tens of thousands of dollars each month. And yet you insist on laying your crimes on the church's doorstep! What are you trying to prove?''

The Joker relaxed a tad. "Oh, is that all? Hey, Joey, baby, that's show biz! You should know that better than anybody. Besides, I like to keep things interesting." He flashed his winning smile. "I get bored so easily."

Droll stared for a long moment at The Joker. My, but the reverend was beginning to get tedious.

"Perhaps you forgot, my dear Joey," The Joker purred, "what you did before I found you? Used cars, I believe? Some of which you made used when you, shall I say, located them on the street? You can always go back to that, you know."

"But you don't understand!" Droll blurted at last. "Why should you mess with such a sweet setup—"

"Because it is *my* setup!" The Joker barked back. "And The Joker likes to play with his things. I have almost everything I need. An inexhaustible supply of money, creative new ways to commit robbery, any number of my own personal batmen—do you know how dull all of this could get? I'm threatened with too much of a good thing!"

"But you could do so much more—"

The Joker shrugged. "Or so much less. But I'll do exactly what I want to do. Now get out of here. And I don't want to see you again unless you're delivering piles and piles of green."

Droll hesitated. "Very well. I'll play it your way. But please remember, Joker, I have resources, too." He turned and left the room.

The Joker folded his gloved hands. Dear, dear. The good reverend seemed to be starting to believe in his own divinity.

Well, very soon now, perhaps The Joker would give old Droll a chance at a resurrection.

Of course, to be resurrected properly, you have to die first.

"Jim!"

"Batman?" Gordon replied.

"I'm glad I caught you before you left." If he ever left, Batman thought but didn't say. "I have word that someone escaped from the church, in part because of a diversion caused by the police search of the building."

"You're sure of that? That's great news. Maybe I'll go home and get some sleep after all."

He woke to Alfred's voice.

"Sir? It's time."

Bruce stretched and rolled out of bed. "Thank you, Alfred." He checked the bedside clock. "I believe I've given myself time for a shower and a light supper."

"Very good, sir."

"And Dick?"

"Ah. Still asleep, sir."

"I see. I do want to talk to him, Alfred. We both said some stupid things before. But I'd guess he needs to recover."

"Yes, sir. I also think that is best."

"Good, Alfred. I think tonight should prove very interesting."

"The Joker, sir?"

"Oh, yes, Alfred, The Joker." Bruce laughed. "The Joker's not going to believe what's going to happen next."

"Ah. *Very* good, sir."

* * *

This place stank. The Joker might have been paying him more money than he'd ever seen before, but Samson still didn't like the smell of fish.

Where was this Bruce Wayne guy, anyway?

It was night when he finally woke up.

Dick took a deep breath and sat up. He was a little dizzy, but besides that, he felt like himself again. A weaker self, like he'd just gotten over a high fever, but it was definitely Dick Grayson under these old PJs Alfred had so thoughtfully provided.

"Ah, Mr. Grayson." Alfred had appeared at the door. Sometimes the way the butler showed up, Dick thought he must have extrasensory perception. "I trust you slept well."

"Like the child I used to be when I lived here," Dick assured him. "Is Bruce around?"

"Unfortunately, no," Alfred replied. "He had an appointment. He asked that you wait for him."

Dick nodded. Was Bruce still avoiding him? Maybe it wouldn't be as easy to talk to him as Dick had hoped.

"Would you care for some supper?" Alfred asked.

That sounded great. One thing he had missed about this drafty old mansion was Alfred's excellent cooking.

"That would be great, Alfred," Dick replied. He swung his legs out and almost fell from the bed. "And then," he added with certainty, "I think I'll go back to bed."

He heard the crash of breaking glass and realized it was the skylight overhead. The Joker stopped, mid-laugh.

Batman let go of his line and landed twenty feet away.

The Joker didn't seem to know what to say. "So soon?" he managed after a moment.

Batman nodded. "You knew, after you left your calling card, that I'd find you. You're surprised that it happened this easily? Come on now. We know each other better than that."

The Joker giggled. "Oh, we do, we do. Why don't you come over and sniff my flower?"

Batman circled him warily. "I'd rather you came over here and took a look at my fist."

The Joker began to circle as well. "A joke? Did Batman make a joke? I thought only The Joker made jokes."

Batman stopped dead. "No more jokes, Joker. I remember what you did to Robin. And for that, I'm going to kill you."

"Have to catch me first!" The Joker bolted for the door. "Nyah, nyah!"

The Joker was fast, but Batman was even faster. They met on the catwalk outside the door, and struggled fifty feet above the ground. The Joker tried to twist around, to spray Batman with acid. But Batman was ready. He ducked out of the way, and The Joker plummeted forward, straight off the catwalk.

Batman started as the drugged dart entered his neck. He slumped backward. One of the boys leaned out of the window to catch him and make sure he didn't follow that Joker down.

What a travesty! What a terrible performance. This would never do! No panache! No soul! No machismo! No sensitivity! No nothing!

The real Joker could only think of one word to sum up his criticism.

"Bleahhh," he remarked.

"Well," the doctor ventured, "when you consider the material we had to work with—"

"True," The Joker admitted. "It was our first attempt. Remember the trouble we had with the first batman? Like the one who strangled himself trying to squeeze out of his cell?" He chuckled. Thinking of a dead "Batman" could always cheer him up. He poked his head out the window. There, some fifty feet down, lay the Joker that had once been Big Mike, lying very still. The Joker whistled. With the way this act ended, it was tough to do an encore.

He turned back to Andrews. "Doctor, you are right as usual. As soon as Samson is done with his present collection, I will give him a very special job."

"Special?" the doctor asked.

But The Joker wasn't telling.

"Let's say I have someone in mind."

PART III

Send in
The Clones

22

Bruce Wayne pulled his sportscar up in front of the main office of the Gotham Fish Company. It was out by the docks, a quarter of the city that was deserted at this time of night. The Joker still knew how to pick his locations.

Bruce checked his watch: 7:45. He was fashionably late. The sort of thing one would expect from a millionaire playboy.

A big, burly fellow in a business suit rushed out from the front door.

"Ah, Mr. Wayne. So good of you to come."

Bruce set the alarm system in his Porsche, then locked the door.

"No trouble."

"I realize this is all a bit unorthodox," the burly fellow said. "You didn't have any trouble finding the place?"

"No trouble," Bruce replied. He noticed the other man made no move to introduce himself.

"Good, good," the other man said. "I think you'll be quite surprised by what we have in store."

"I don't know about that," Bruce answered as he followed the other man inside. "I don't surprise easily."

Finally Wayne had arrived. Samson just wanted to get this over with.

The whole setup was a bit more elaborate than the kind he usually liked. For some reason it had taken The Joker more effort than usual to get this place cleared out. And Samson decided he needed help. Samson hated to cut anybody in on the action, but sometimes, especially in a place as big as this, assistants were necessary. Besides, his information told him that Wayne was athletically built and fast on his feet. Usually, Samson could take these guys just with the element of surprise, but it didn't hurt to have an extra pair of fists around.

So all he had to do now was wait for George to bring the mark around.

"You!" somebody yelled behind him.

What the hell was this? Samson spun around. It was some guy in a guard's uniform. The Joker's information hadn't told him about any watchmen.

"What are you doing here?" the watchmen demanded. "Don't you know this is holy property?"

Uh-oh. Even worse. This wasn't any ordinary watchman. This was one of Droll's crazies.

"Hey," Samson said in a low voice. "Reverend Droll sent me to take a look around. I'm sort of a safety inspector."

But the crazy was having none of it. "Liar! You are an enemy of the Joke! The Reverend Droll must be—"

There was a soft thunk as Samson shot him. The crazy fell over, quiet at last. Jeez. Didn't these religious guys have any sense of humor?

But now Samson had no time to get rid of the body. He would have to jump Wayne the minute George brought him into the room, before their latest victim had any chance to get suspicious.

Maybe, Samson thought, he should retire from this sort of thing. And maybe he just would, after he got to do Gordon.

Bruce's guide led him into the interior of the plant. He kept up a constant line of patter.

"My superiors are waiting for you up in the office. They've put out quite a spread for you." He chuckled appreciatively. "You'd never believe how many kinds of fish they've got! Since I've got to take you through the plant to get there anyway, they suggested I give you a little bit of a tour."

Bruce wondered where this guy came from. His spiel was almost good enough to be believable. He probably spent most of his time talking little old ladies out of their social security checks.

"Now, if you'll just follow me," the guide said as he turned left, "I'll show you the processing plant."

There was another noise up ahead that had nothing to do with processing. Someone was screaming about a joke, and the Reverend Droll. The noise cut off abruptly after a sharp sound that might have been a muffled gunshot.

His guide smiled apologetically. "A little trouble with

the help," the burly man explained. "It's so difficult to get people to clean fish these days."

Bruce thought they'd be more professional than this. Apparently they had found it so easy to abduct Gotham City's leading citizens, they were getting sloppy. He decided it was time to get his guide to work for his pay.

"I'm sorry," he said as he stopped abruptly. "I don't think I have the time for a tour of your plant. The invitation said your superiors were willing to make me a very substantial offer. I'm not the sort of person to be kept waiting. If I do not hear the offer within the next two minutes, I'm leaving."

"Of course, of course, we certainly don't want to waste your time." The guide bustled over and grabbed Bruce's arm. That was perfect. Bruce had him just where he wanted him. "It's really not that far. Just through that door up ahead."

The door up ahead? That's where the others would be waiting. It was nice of his guide to tell him. Bruce took a deep breath, readying himself for action.

"Right through here," the guide instructed as he slowed his step. They wanted Bruce to go in here first.

It was a shame he wouldn't oblige. He grabbed on to the guide's arm and fell away from him, using his weight to pull the startled man around and in front of him.

A man came out of the shadows ahead. The man held a gun. Bruce threw the two men together. The man with the gun yelled and tried to regain his balance, while Bruce's guide fell to the floor.

They'd expect Bruce to run now. So Bruce did the unexpected—he ran straight toward them.

He hit the gunman's wrists with the flat of his hand, and the gun went flying across the room. The guide, though, was trying to get up underneath them. Bruce stepped back as arms tried to tackle him from down below.

The former gunman tried to circle behind him and grab for his neck. He gave the gunman an elbow in the stomach, then kicked out forward to catch the guide's chin. He turned just in time to avoid a roundhouse right from the gunman, and landed a right and left of his own. The gunman staggered back, banging against a gleaming metal machine.

But the guide had managed to get back up on his feet. He roared as he came for Bruce, as if his voice were somehow going to give him strength. Bruce tried to side-step his charge, but the guide shifted his direction, too, while both his fists flailed wildly in Bruce's direction. This kind of attack couldn't do Bruce much harm, but it certainly kept him busy. Where was the other man?

Bruce decided he didn't have time to wonder. He felled the guide with a single well-placed punch to the jaw, then spun around, ready for the attack. It didn't come. The other man was already on the far side of the room, running the other way.

The second one was going to get away. Bruce wished he had access to Batman's utility belt; he would have had half a dozen ways to stop the other man without any problem. Sometimes leading this double life could be nothing but problems.

He ran across the room, but he knew by the time he reached the doorway, and saw the long white hall full of windows and doors, that he had lost his quarry. Well, he had one for a keepsake. That would have to do. It was so quiet down here by the docks at this time of night, no one should see him load a limp body into the passenger seat of his Porsche.

*   *   *

The Reverend Droll knew he had pushed The Joker too far. But what else could he have done?

First off, The Joker was crazy. Brilliantly crazy, but crazy nonetheless. Why else would he build up such a fantastic criminal organization, and then spend the rest of his time trying to find ways to jeopardize it?

He had to take steps to protect himself. Droll would no longer cooperate with all of The Joker's schemes. He'd already told his followers that they should no longer automatically obey the orders of The Joker's men.

Still, he could not force out the man who had created the church in the first place. And The Joker was a powerful man. It would not do to anger him unnecessarily.

Unless he decided to take measures even crazier than those of The Joker. Perhaps it was time to remove The Joker first, before The Joker had any thoughts of removing Droll. And by setting him up as the head of the church, The Joker had unwittingly given Droll the perfect weapon to destroy his employer.

But he had to protect himself first. It was time to go to the authorities and give them just enough information to implicate The Joker, and guarantee the Reverend Droll an honored spot in this community for years to come.

Now that was a joke worth laughing about.

23

_____

The Joker smashed a chair through the window. He felt like smashing things. Small things, big things, maybe even living things.

"You didn't get him? A perfectly good multimillionaire, and he slips through your fingers? And I wasn't even going to make him the Batman." Dr. Andrews ducked as The Joker grabbed a second chair. "No, I considered Bruce Wayne good enough to be—a Joker!" The second chair followed the first. "There were two of you, up against a member of the effete upper class! Is *everyone* around here incompetent?"

"Man," said Samson from where The Joker had backed him into a corner, "you don't understand. He was everywhere! He beat George to a bloody pulp!"

The Joker stopped throwing things. The others in the room grew very quiet. My, that reaction was gratifying;

gratifying enough that he didn't need to kill anybody just now.

"But The Joker can turn aside his wrath," he said charitably. "The Joker can know forgiveness. Samson, I will give you one more chance." He smiled graciously. "And, yes, you get to do Gordon!"

"Gordon?" The look of fear in Samson's eyes turned to one of wonder. "Gee, boss, that's great! I won't let you down this time."

"No, of course you won't," The Joker agreed amiably. "No one ever lets The Joker down twice. And I have big plans for Commissioner Gordon. The sooner he is in my hands, the better I will like it."

"Yessir!" Samson agreed. The Joker stepped back, and Samson scurried from the room.

The Joker made a soft *tsking* sound deep in his acid-scarred throat. It was such a shame about Samson. He had seemed so competent when all he was snatching was overweight businessmen and aging public officials. At the first challenge, though, he completely fell apart.

Oh, well. The Joker had been planning to eliminate Samson anyway. And The Joker knew he always made the right decisions.

Batman pulled his car over to the curb. He shook the other man's shoulder.

"Good morning."

The burly man blinked and focused his eyes. There was a gratifying look of fear in his eyes. "Batman?"

"Pleased to meet you."

The burly man tried to struggle, but his bonds were too tight.

"Oh, shit," he muttered. "I've got to get out of here. How'd I end up with Batman?"

Batman smiled over at his captive passenger. "I gave Bruce Wayne some pointers."

"You were helping Wayne?" The burly man flexed his jaw. "No wonder he won."

"Oh, Bruce Wayne can take care of himself," Batman reassured the crook. "And in return, Mr. Wayne gave you to me."

"Gave me?" The fear was back in the other man's eyes.

"It was the least he could do. You see, I have a certain interest in your employer."

"M-Mr. Samson?" the burly man stuttered. "All I know is that he collects people—"

Batman slammed the flat of his hand against the dashboard. "I don't care about the small fry like Samson. I want to know who both of you were working for."

The burly man leaned as far away as his bonds would let him. "But I can't tell you about that! He'd kill me!"

Batman regarded his prisoner for a moment. "And I won't?"

"Oh, Jesus," the burly man whispered. He made small animal noises, like a squirrel with his tail caught in a trap, as Batman reached for him. The noises increased as Batman dragged the man toward him, becoming more shrill and hysterical. The man jerked back and forth, but he really had no place to go in the confines of the car.

"You will tell me what I need to know, now," Batman said quietly, "or I will stop being nice to you."

The burly man gave one final, guttural scream, and then was quiet. He had stopped struggling, too. Batman realized that he had passed out.

Well, Batman thought, at least he hadn't done any permanent physical damage to him. He pushed the limp body back into the passenger seat. He really was afraid, with the anger he still held inside him; afraid that, for maybe the first time in his whole career, he might go too far. It was better that he let Gordon and the department handle this one.

He got out of the Batmobile, then walked over to the other side of the car and removed the unconscious felon, throwing the criminal over his shoulder like the sack of refuse that he was.

No one spoke to him as he strode across the lobby and rode the elevator up to Gordon's office. Ms. Davis raised her eyebrows appreciatively as Batman passed her desk. He knocked on Gordon's door with his free hand.

"Come," Gordon's voice replied.

He opened the door and walked in with his burden.

"Batman?"

"I brought you a present." Batman set the limp form down in a nearby chair.

"I see." Gordon waved at the new but still unconscious addition. "I assume this has a story to go along with the body?"

"This is one of the kidnappers. I caught him in the act." Batman briefly outlined how he had set up his trap with the aid of Bruce Wayne.

Gordon shook his head. "I'm getting nothing but surprises." He held out a piece of paper. "Look at this fax that was just delivered to me."

Batman took the paper and read the hastily typed paragraph on the page before him.

"Commisioner Gordn: We must speak. I have information about criminal acttivities and people who are trying to discredit my chucrh. The fate of Gotham City is at stake! But we must meet alone! I will be at my seventh street church at 4 p.m. today. Please. I will only talk to you if you are alone. We cannot trust anybody. J. Droll"

"What do you make of it?" Gordon asked. "Besides the fact that the man can't type?"

Batman looked back at the fax in his hands. Actually, the typing errors gave the page a certain authenticity.

"It could be genuine," he said at last.

"Is it a trap?" Gordon asked.

Batman considered the question. "Maybe. Or maybe he's trying to double-cross The Joker."

"Exactly my thoughts on the matter," Gordon agreed. "And if that's the case, I have to go."

Batman nodded at his old friend. He would do no differently in the same situation. "You may go in there alone. But I won't be very far away."

The phone beeped at him as he reentered the Batmobile.

"Bruce?" Dick's voice said on the other end of the line.

"Finally up?" Batman replied.

"Yeah," Dick replied, and Batman thought he could still hear exhaustion in the other man's voice. "I've got a lot to tell you about Droll's organization."

"Maybe I'll have something to tell you, too," Batman countered. "Gordon's on his way to have a meeting with him."

"Meeting?" There was fear in Dick's voice now. "No, that's too dangerous." What, Batman wondered, had happened to Dick inside that church?

"I'll be watching him," Batman said reassuringly.

"Listen, you know that we've handled much worse than renegade ministers in our day. Get Alfred to fix you something to eat. I'll check in with you as soon as this is over."

He hung up the phone before Dick could object. The young man needed to rest. And soon, Dick Grayson and Bruce Wayne would talk.

Dick had left some old clothes in his closet. His chest and arms had filled out some in the years he'd been away from here, but he found what once had been a loose-fitting sweatshirt and an old pair of jeans that didn't need a belt. He had to get out of here. Bruce and the commissioner didn't realize what they were getting into.

"Master Grayson?" the butler called as Dick hurried down the stairs. "Would you care for some dinner?"

"Sorry, Alfred," Dick called as he ran to one of the hidden panels that led to the Batcave. "I have to go."

"But, Master Dick—" The butler's voice cut off as the panel closed between them. Dick hurried into the garage. Thank goodness Bruce still kept a motorcycle down here. Maybe, just maybe, Dick could be in time to keep anything serious from happening.

This was really interesting. After this, The Joker would never yell at him again. Hell, after this, The Joker would give him a promotion!

Sure he had messed up, and worse than he ever had before. He admitted it—it had really shaken him. And The Joker's crazy reaction had shaken him worse.

But Samson always thought ahead. That's how he had stayed alive as long as he had. But who knew that tapping the reverend's fax line would yield such positive results? And at just the right time, too?

"Commisioner Gordn: We must speak. I have information about criminal acttivities and people who are trying to discredit my chucrh."

Hoo-boy. Was The Joker going to love to hear about this!

"The fate of Gotham City is at stake!"

And the fate of a lot more than that, Drolly boy.

"But we must meet alone!"

How convenient. It was almost as if Droll were still working for him!

"I will be at my seventh street church at 4 p.m. today. Please. I will only talk to you if you are alone. We cannot trust anybody."

You can say that again.

"J. Droll"

So Samson was going to get to grab Gordon and bump off Droll at the same time? Two for the price of one! Yeah! He was going to get a goddamn promotion for sure!

24

Gordon stopped his car in front of the church. The street around him was very quiet for this hour of the afternoon. Of course, in this industrially depressed corner of town there probably never was all that much business. There were a couple of warehouses across the street from the church that looked like they'd been abandoned for years. Still, what had happened to all of Droll's busy congregation? Were they all out someplace hawking flowers?

Gordon wondered if it might have been wise to make some sort of counterproposal to using the church as a meeting place. But, in trying to find some neutral ground, he might have lost any information that the Reverend Droll might be willing to give—information that would stop the kidnappings, and these so-called Batman murders, once and for all.

The commissioner took a deep breath before he climbed the church steps. There really was nothing out here in the street. Perhaps that in itself was a sign, but of what? That Reverend Droll had warned everybody away? Or that Droll, or The Joker, had men hiding somewhere, waiting for the right moment to shoot or kidnap him?

Even though he couldn't see him, at least Gordon knew Batman was with him on this one. Gordon just hoped all this was worth it.

If not, he and Batman would have to fight their way out.

Damn!

Gordon had parked his car in the exact wrong position. There was no way Samson could get off a clear shot. Come on. Move over in front of the car. Take a look around. It's just a tranquilizer dart. Won't hurt at all. One quick pain, like a bee sting, really, and next thing you know you'll be in the arms of The Joker.

But Gordon only stood in front of his car. So close. And there was nothing Samson could do about it.

This sort of thing only happened when you had to make all your plans at the last minute. Samson couldn't believe his luck when he'd found the abandoned warehouse directly across from the Church of Perpetual Happiness. It was luckier still, what with that missing pane of glass in the warehouse door. Only a small pane of glass, but plenty large enough for a rifle with a tranquilizer dart. Heck, he even got his car inside with him.

All he had to do is give Gordon one quick shot, then take the car out there and pick him up. What could be simpler?

Samson realized now there had been too much luck. Too many easy answers. And now he had an all-too-simple problem.

With the car in the way, the missing pane of glass was just a bit too low for Samson to shoot Gordon anyplace but in the head. Wouldn't you know that, this time at least, Samson didn't want to do that kind of damage? After all, he needed to deliver Gordon more or less in one piece. That's the only way The Joker could have his fun.

And Gordon was going to stand out there forever, just out of reach. Samson looked around. When he had cased this place a minute ago, he had seen a stairway next to what must have once been the office. That would do it. As long as the stairs weren't rotten, he could get up there and get off a clean shot.

Samson moved quickly. The stairs groaned beneath him as he climbed, but they didn't give. There was another window up here on the landing. That should be perfect. Samson put his rifle to his shoulder as he peered out the dirty pane.

But Gordon was gone. While Samson was climbing the stairs, the cop must have gone into the church.

Samson cursed. He didn't dare follow Gordon in there. Who knew how many people and what sort of traps Droll had waiting inside? But when Gordon came back out—if Gordon came back out—Samson would drop him before he got off the church steps.

This time, Batman had found a place he could watch from without being disturbed. At first, he had even thought that Droll had stayed true to his word, and had removed all his followers from the immediate area. But once he had reached the roof of the church, he spotted first a pair, and then two more pairs, of Droll's followers out in the woods surrounding the back and sides of the church.

Of course, the possibility existed that Droll always kept a few people on the grounds for security reasons, and all six of them were some distance from the church. The reverend might still be holding to his end of the bargain for the meeting. But, then again, it depended on Droll's definition of "security." If Droll had people out here in the open like this, how many more might he have inside?

Batman opened his utility belt and removed a device that looked a bit like an oversize stethoscope. If, as he hoped, Gordon and Droll met in one of the main rooms below him, he should be able to hear every word of the conversation.

Then if anything sounded wrong, he could make his move.

It was a gamble. But before he had become a reverend, Joe Drolowsky had had a bit of experience with gambling.

He had always been good with words, whether it was in selling swampland to retired couples or convincing the judge that, no, he'd never think of skipping bail in a million years.

Now, though, he had to be better with words than he had ever been before. Not that it was that difficult to convince a cop. Most policemen would believe anything, as long as you were ratting on someone and they could get credit for the collar.

No, but he had to make this story stick, so that he could both get rid of The Joker and stay squeaky clean himself. This was one town he couldn't leave in the middle of the night. This setup was too sweet. The money was too good, and it could only get better. And, hell, unless you took a good look inside it, it smelled as legitimate as your grand-mother!

He guessed he should thank The Joker and that weird doctor of his for clueing him into the way this psycholog-ical brainwashing thing worked. Hey, he might even be able to find a place for the doctor in his organization, as long as the shrink could take orders.

As for The Joker, well, The Joker never took orders from anybody. Too bad. From now on, the Reverend Droll didn't take orders, either.

The Joker didn't know it, but he had finally met some-body more ruthless than he was.

Gordon stepped inside the church.

"Ah, Commissioner," a voice said from the next room. "So good of you to come."

Gordon walked through the next doorway, into that large, empty chapel that had had all of its pews removed. There were two chairs in the middle of the great expanse of floor. Reverend Droll, wearing a business suit, sat in one. He waved for Gordon to join him in the other.

"Come now, Commissioner. We need to get to busi-ness. Both of us are busy men." He smiled graciously as Gordon approached. "You'll forgive these rather extraor-dinary steps I've taken to speak to you, but once you know who we're dealing with, I'm sure you'll understand."

Gordon sat in the other chair. He, too, wanted to make this as short as possible.

"Fine," he said. "Tell me what I need to know."

The smile fell from Droll's face. "I am afraid that I have some connections to The Joker."

"Really?" Gordon replied. Even though the police al-ready had this information, it was interesting to hear it from the lips of the minister. Maybe Gordon would get something worthwhile out of this after all.

Droll nodded dourly. "Yes, and once you're associated with The Joker, it's very difficult to become, shall we say, unassociated?"

"I would imagine so," Gordon replied noncommittally. "What, exactly, is the nature of this involvement?"

"We are paying for The Joker's protection," Droll replied smoothly. "In the early days of the church, when we were small and weak, there were certain unscrupulous elements that wanted to turn our organization from the good deeds that we do."

More unscrupulous than Droll? Gordon thought, but he said nothing aloud.

"We needed help—we were offered help from what we thought was a legitimate source, until we found that the cure we had picked was worse than the disease!"

"Are you talking blackmail?" Gordon asked.

"One of the basic tenets of our church, Commissioner, is forgiveness. We do not research the past lives of our members. They start their lives anew once they join the church. Unfortunately, some of the credit agencies and lending institutions we do business with are not so lenient. The Joker—" The reverend let the rest of the sentence drop.

"Tell me, Reverend," Gordon replied. "What did you do before becoming a minister?"

Droll's expressive eyebrows rose in surprise. "Like the rest of my flock, since I have joined the church, I have no past."

Gordon didn't particularly like this double-speak. "I'm not sure that I can help you."

"Why, of course you can, Commissioner," Droll said

as his smile returned. "We know you'd like to catch those who break the law."

On that, Gordon thought, at least they were agreed.

"Then what can I do for you?" he asked again.

"I have names and numbers," Droll said. "Meeting places where we are supposed to deliver our protection money." He reached into the inner pocket of his suit coat and pulled out a long white envelope. "I thought the police could use that information to find The Joker."

"Perhaps we could," Gordon said as he accepted the envelope.

"You'll have to forgive my need for secrecy," Droll continued. "There is one very important fact that I have learned in dealing with this man: The Joker has associates everywhere—even, forgive me, in the police department."

"Really?" Gordon asked. "What else can you tell me?"

"I have only heard rumors," Droll admitted. "And threats. The Joker is very good at threats."

Gordon didn't trust this man for a minute. He was sure this so-called minister knew far more than he was telling, and was in far closer to The Joker than he would dare to admit.

Still, thanks to Droll, Gordon had some names and dates. Maybe these would help the police catch The Joker.

But Gordon wanted to catch the Reverend Droll as well.

He had come here so quickly, he had barely had time to think.

Dick pulled the motorcycle up in front of the church. There was nobody out here. What should he do now?

The obvious move would be to go inside the church.

He tried to get off the bike, but he was shaking too much to move.

No. Dick swallowed, but his throat still felt far too dry. He felt that if he took one step inside that church, he'd never get out again.

It was the fear inside him talking. The fear of losing himself. He was in worse shape than he thought. Maybe Bruce had been right about him staying home and resting.

But Bruce was around here someplace, too. Not to mention Commissioner Gordon. And both of them were in danger.

As long as he was here, he had to take a look around.

He just wouldn't set foot inside the church.

Batman heard the motorcycle pull up in front of the church. Maybe this was Droll's way of making his move. He pulled off his listening device and took the three steps to the edge of the roof.

He didn't believe what he saw next. What was Dick doing here? Did he have some information that they needed? Batman didn't want to give away his position, in case someone was watching what went on down below. Could he trust Dick to stay out of trouble for another minute?

Batman guessed he had to.

Dick walked slowly around the side of the church. He saw no sign of Batman, or anyone else.

"Dick!" It was a woman's voice, calling softly. He turned in the direction of the noise.

He froze. It was Sharon.

"Dick?" She took a step toward him. "Why did you leave us?"

No. He couldn't face up to this. He had come back here too soon. He had to get away from this.

He ran back toward the front of the church.

This was getting a little too interesting for Samson's tastes.

For a minute there, he was afraid he was going to have to take out that guy on the motorcycle. But the guy had disappeared behind the church right away. Samson had no idea what that meant. And he didn't want to know. Come on, Gordon. Come back out. These things always seemed to take forever.

Wait a moment. Samson thought he saw movement. He raised the rifle. One shot, one pop, and his life would be fulfilled.

Dick ran for all he was worth.

Dick didn't know why he was looking at the warehouse across the street. He probably wanted to be looking at anything but the church.

Dick saw movement in the window as he rounded the corner. He realized it was a man holding a rifle. He turned to look at the church steps at last, and saw Commissioner Gordon walking out the door.

"Jim!" he yelled. "Gordon! Watch out!"

The commissioner stopped and stared at him. Dick ran up the steps. He had to get him out of the way.

He felt a sharp pain in his neck.

This wasn't his day.

Gordon had jumped back into the church, and the other guy had taken the sleeping dart instead. Well, Samson guessed he was going to have to go in and get him. He jumped down the stairs and threw open his car door, throwing the rifle onto the passenger seat beside him. At least the car was pointing the right way. He floored the gas and drove straight through the warehouse's rotting front door, screeching to a halt by the sleeping stranger. He jumped out of the car.

"Samson!" somebody yelled. "Stop where you are!"

What? Who knew his name? The voice came from overhead.

Samson didn't like what he saw next. It was Batman.

It was time for Samson to cut his losses and get the hell out of here. But he didn't dare go back to The Joker empty-handed. He threw open the passenger door of the car, grabbed the sleeping man, and hauled him in next to the rifle.

Then he hauled ass. Gordon would have to wait for another day.

25

The Joker couldn't believe this.

"No Gordon?"

Samson tried to explain. It was all Gordon this and Batman that. How could The Joker have ever trusted somebody as weak as this? Samson even seemed to be backing away as he spoke. What, did he expect somebody to be angry?

"Well," The Joker said magnanimously. "You've brought me a fine, strong young man. We'll make *him* The Joker instead!"

Samson exhaled and smiled. "Oh. Good. Glad I could be of service."

"My dear Samson," The Joker added. "You'll never know the true depth of that service. Don't worry. You'll get your reward."

It was, after all, time to do a little something with Samson, too.

He turned to the doctor. "Isn't it about time for our rounds?" He so looked forward to visiting his batmen, all four of them. The strong, silent type. The poet in a cape. The fellow who was going to grind The Joker to pulp. And, of course, the newest Batman, who was the best one yet.

Of course, The Joker had yet to tell the doctor how they were going to make their rounds more interesting still.

Where was he?

One moment he had been rushing out to meet Commissioner Gordon in front of the Church of Perpetual Happiness. Then, blackness.

Dick had woken up in a cell. He had manacles around his wrists, with those manacles attached by chains to the wall behind his cot. Whoever had trapped him didn't want him going anywhere. Somehow, though, this didn't feel like the church's doing. For one thing, this setup cost money, and Dick didn't think Reverend Droll spent anything, except on Reverend Droll.

They must have noticed he was up and around about fifteen minutes after he was awake. That's when the videos began. A panel high in the wall whirred aside to show a large screen above his cot, a screen on which was shown newsreel footage of The Joker. Was The Joker involved in this? It was either that, or somebody who wanted to use The Joker.

Dick had seen most of these films before. Besides Batman, he probably knew The Joker better than anybody else on this side of the law. Of course, whoever had him trapped here wouldn't know that, would they? Maybe he could use that to his advantage.

There was sound, too, most of it news commentary, but some of it apparently an interview with The Joker, where he talked of "pride in his exploits." And every once in a while, a voice would boom, "*You* are The Joker!"

Who was The Joker? Dick didn't get it.

"Ah," a sarcastic voice spoke behind him. "Lost in our studies, are we?"

Dick turned around to see two men standing on the other side of the bars. Well, here was one answer—and he was sure he'd learn the rest far too soon.

One of the men was The Joker.

Oh, The Joker was in one of the very best moods.

"So, what do you think of our newest addition?"

For some reason the good doctor was not so enthusiastic. "In an odd sort of way, he seems to know you."

"Is that all?" He giggled. "Everyone knows The Joker."

But the good doctor only scratched at his beard in a distracted sort of way. "No, no, I mean he knows you personally."

The Joker still couldn't see the doctor's objection. "Well, that's good, isn't it? Soon, he will know me *very* personally."

"I suppose so," the doctor said, his voice still not filled with enthusiasm. "It was just a feeling I had."

"Perhaps he's a particularly sensitive lad," The Joker said brightly. "That would be for the best. We do need him quickly."

The doctor considered. "I can have him ready in— say—two weeks?"

"Oh, dear, dear, no, that will never do." The Joker waved a gloved finger in the doctor's face. "Not soon enough. I need him within seven days. They're closing in on us, Doctor. It would be a shame if this little drama lacked a final act."

Now the doctor looked really upset. "Seven days? The surgery alone—"

"I quite agree," The Joker answered. "Surgery is out of the question. But there must be other ways to make our young charge a bit more—Jokeresque."

The doctor sighed. "There are certain drugs that will cause a temporary rictus of the facial muscles. If administered properly, it will approximate your smile. Not quite as—" He paused, as if groping for the proper word.

"Grand?" The Joker replied. "Was that the word you were trying to come up with? Or perhaps 'dramatic'?"

"Most certainly," the doctor said in a distracted way that showed his mind was elsewhere. "The rest can be done with dyes and cosmetics. Yes, I think we can come up with a good approximation. He can be physically ready in seven days. But mentally?"

"I depend upon you, Doctor."

The Joker chuckled merrily.

It would never end.

Video images flashed on the screen in front of him. Most of them were of common things: news leaders, personalities, domestic scenes, and every once in a while a shot of The Joker.

Every time he saw The Joker, the electricity shot through Dick's body.

He had tried to turn away, to not follow the images, but it was no use. The electricity came whether he was watch-

ing the monitor or not. The manacles he wore were wired.
There was no way he could escape it. He decided at last
to pay attention to the images being screened for his benefit. Then when he saw The Joker's face, at least he could
be prepared for what was coming.

The video monitor showed scenes from fast-food res-
taurants.

It was so strange that something like this should happen
so soon after his experience with the church—almost as
if his experiences there were a rehearsal for what was
happening now. But in the church, they attacked his mind.
Now, The Joker was attacking his body.

He started to laugh. It was funny really, in a horrible
sort of way.

The Joker showed up on the screen, but Dick couldn't
stop laughing.

There was no shock.

Dick laughed even louder. Maybe they were messing
with his brain after all.

The monitor showed popular film stars. Dick kept on
laughing. Then The Joker again, and still no shock.

The monitor showed a picture of Batman.

Laughter turned to a scream as electricity surged through
his body.

The voltage surge left him gasping for air. He closed
his eyes. He couldn't watch the video monitor anymore.
He had thought, when he escaped from the church, that
nothing could be any worse.

He was wrong.

Now he was in hell.

Dick had disappeared again, and no one was talking.
Batman would not allow this to happen.

Gordon was working on the man Batman had picked up at the fish-processing warehouse. They had found out his name—George Bernoff. And he would talk, about Samson. They knew a lot about Samson. And three days into the questioning, he had finally admitted to knowing that Samson was associated with The Joker. Gordon swore Bernoff would crack at any time, and they'd learn everything.

Anytime. What could happen to Dick while they were waiting for "any time." *What had happened to Jason?*

"Excuse me, sir?"

Batman turned from his computer screen to look at Alfred.

"Since you have not been coming up to the house much in these last few days, I took it upon myself to come down here," Alfred said. "You see, I have been thinking, and I believe some of my conversations with Master Dick could be pertinent to the case."

Batman sat up. "Yes, Alfred?"

"Well, this concerns The Joker, and that church," the butler continued. "Master Dick did tell me a little bit about his experience, sir. And, as I recalled, you had mentioned that the leader of the church, the Reverend Droll, might have some clue as to The Joker's whereabouts."

"That's true, Alfred. But Droll hides in that church of his. We haven't been able to get a fix on Droll's whereabouts since the night he met with Gordon."

"Ah, but that's where Dick's knowledge comes in handy. In the conversations we had over supper, he mentioned a point of interest about the reverend's itinerary concerning that old church building. Apparently, Droll addresses that particular flock every Thursday."

"Thursday?" Batman asked.

"Tomorrow, sir."

It was true. Sometimes he did lose track of the time.

"At seven P.M.," the butler added.

"Alfred, that's wonderful." If Droll hadn't changed his pattern, he and Batman were going to have a little talk.

Batman smiled.

26

Droll's car stopped abruptly.

"Fred?" he called to his driver. "Is something the matter, Fred?"

His driver didn't reply. Droll peered out of the tinted glass of the nearest window. The sun had disappeared behind the warehouses, but there was still enough light to see. They had almost reached the church, but, for some reason, had stopped about half a block short.

"Fred?" He rapped on the glass that separated the driver's seat from the rear compartment. Fred still didn't answer.

Droll opened the compartment beneath the back seat and took out his .44. He looked back out the tinted glass, but could see no movement at all. Could his driver have had a heart attack? Fred had been a good driver. This was most inconvenient. He decided he would have to check.

He unlocked the door. The door jerked out of his hands as it swung open.

Batman stood there.

"It's time we talked," Batman said.

"I don't have anything to say to you!" Droll brought up the .44 to protect himself. There was a sharp pain in his wrist. The .44 fell from his numb fingers.

Batman sat next to him, his boot on top of Droll's gun. Batman closed the door.

"I don't like to repeat myself," Batman said. "You have some information that I need."

Who did this guy think he was? Batman or not, he wasn't going to get anything out of Joey. "Information? I'm only a poor servant—"

He found Batman's face very close to his. "Don't give me that. I know the scam you're running. The police know the scam you're running. I also know you're in it with The Joker."

Droll tried to push away, but Batman had too tight a grip on his robes. It was too close in here, too dark. Why had he wanted to ride in a limousine anyway?

"He—" Droll managed to reply, "he told you that?"

"It's one of the things I know," Batman answered. "But there's another thing that I don't know. If you tell me that, I might even let you go. I might be really generous, and give you twenty-four hours to get out of town."

He might get out of this? Droll swallowed. He had to stop and think, figure out what the best angle was for him. "Well, The Joker's got a lot of hideouts. I want to cooperate! I told the police commissioner about some of them when—"

Batman shook him again. "The Joker has a headquarters. You know where that is."

"Uh, yes," Droll whispered. "It's underground, one of those places that was never completed—"

The door behind Batman opened with a clunk.

"It's the reverend!" somebody yelled.

"The reverend!" a hundred voices took up the call.

Droll clammed up. His flock had come to rescue him.

So close. Batman should have taken Droll someplace quiet, away from his zombie followers.

They had swarmed into the car, like lemmings drawn to Droll. Batman had grabbed the minister and pushed his way out the far side. But the flock was there, too. Most of them were scrawny, and they didn't have much strength, but there were so many of them, and they pressed forward with a dogged tenacity, as if they didn't care what happened to them so long as they rescued their beloved reverend.

"Get away from him!" a voice shouted. "I've got a gun!"

Batman saw that one of the reverend's followers held his .44. The follower closed his eyes as he pulled the trigger. Batman ducked. The reverend screamed. The bullet had got him in the shoulder.

A great wailing sound rose from the followers as they surged forward to surround Batman and the reverend.

There were hands all over him as they pulled Droll away, hands tearing at his suit and face. Batman pressed a button at his belt as he grabbed the line he had set before, and let himself be pulled above the crowd, back to the roof of the warehouse. Once he had his feet solidly beneath him, he looked back to the crowd. No one was following him, but there would be no way now to get back at Droll. His followers had encircled him a hundred strong, and were leading him back toward the church. He would learn no more from the reverend tonight.

Underground, Droll had said. A place never completed. Batman had an idea about that, but he had to do a little more research first.

He called Gordon as soon as he got back to the Bat-mobile.

"Droll confessed to me that he's working for The Joker," Batman explained. "I think he's going to make a break for it soon. You should send a couple of your men down to the Third Street church to tail him. I think he'll lead you to a great deal of The Joker's money, very soon."

Gordon said he'd get right on it.

"Any luck with Bernoff?"

Not yet. Gordon had left the interrogation room to talk to Batman.

"I can't wait any longer," Batman replied. "I need information from him. I'm coming over, now." He broke the connection.

Underground, Batman thought. A place never completed. He had another question for Gordon, once he got to City Hall.

Batman could have found The Joker all along. He had just been looking at the wrong records.

"So they completed the underground complex first?"

Building Inspector John MacPhee peered over his glasses and nodded. "They would have had to. If you look at these blueprints, you'll see that the four major towers all rise from the corners of the complex. It was designed to act as the foundation for the whole place. The place probably went bankrupt before they could put a lot of the amenities in, but they would have had a good solid concrete shell, with air ducts and fans, probably a heating system, water, electricity.''

Batman couldn't think of a better hideout. There was only one nagging question. "But the property went bankrupt. A bank must own it now. How do they keep bank officials, or prospective buyers, from finding out their secret?''

"I wondered about that, too," Gordon agreed. "I did a little research while you and Johnny were looking at the plans. Called up the title on the computer. Another company bought the property from the First Gotham Bank months ago, but for some reason never removed the old condominium signs. Heavenly Properties Limited is the name of the company.''

"Heavenly Properties?" Batman asked. Could it be that obvious?

It was Gordon's turn to nod. "A wholly owned subsidiary of the Gotham Fish Company. Or, as my aging grandmother is so fond of saying: Bingo.''

Of course. If The Joker could, he'd pull off something right in your face. He led Batman straight to that condominium so that he could laugh at him. Well, someone else was going to be laughing now.

Batman stood. "Commissioner. I think we have a little trip in our future.''

"I'd say so," Gordon replied. "But won't The Joker be waiting for us?''

"No doubt." Batman pointed down at the blueprint. "But we've got the general layout of the place. And I have a feeling a certain gentleman of our acquaintance can fill us in on some of the specifics.''

*   *   *

"You're doing what?"

Poor George. His eyes were bulging so far out of his head, Batman half expected them to pop out and roll away.

"Giving you back to Batman," Gordon said with a remarkably straight face. "After all, he only loaned you to us."

"Loaned?" George squawked. "What does that mean? You can't just give me away!"

Gordon shrugged. "You wouldn't talk. We gave you your chance. It's out of my hands."

"The police can't just give away a prisoner!" George wailed. "It just—isn't done!"

"What are you talking about?" Gordon looked at the other policemen in the room. "Any of you guys know who this fellow is? Batman never brought anybody in here. After all, the police department doesn't cooperate with masked vigilantes."

"Come on, George," Batman said as he grabbed the prisoner's arm. "We're going away." He pulled George behind him into the elevator down to the garage. The elevator door closed.

For a long moment there was nothing but the soft hum of machinery.

George couldn't stand it. "What happens now?"

"One of two things," Batman replied simply. "You answer my questions, or—"

"Or?"

"You join all those other stubborn people who wouldn't cooperate."

George pressed his back against the doors, as far away from Batman as he could get. "You can't! We're in police headquarters!"

"We're in an elevator now, George. And officially, you no longer exist."

Batman smiled.

"All right. I worked for The Joker. Not all the time. Off and on? What do you want?"

"Does the word 'condominium' mean anything to you? River Point Condominiums?"

George hesitated. Batman stepped forward and punched the stop button.

The elevator stopped.

"The hideout?" George blurted. "I'll tell you how to get in. Oh, God. Just don't kill me."

George cowered as Batman moved toward him. Batman reached past his shoulder to press the down button a second time. The elevator whirred to life.

"Who said anything about killing?" Batman asked. "George, I think you're starting to exist all over again."

This had gone too far. Joey Droll was in danger. And he was bleeding.

The members of his flock talked about sending for a doctor. The reverend acquiesced, as long as the doctor was a member of the congregation. It might take a little longer to get one of the two doctors who belonged over here, but think of all the messy paperwork and official questions it would avoid.

In the meantime, Joey had to give a speech.

"Brethren!" he called. "Let us all go into the chapel together! I have important words that I must share with you!"

His flock followed as he walked across the chapel and climbed behind the podium.

"My fellow believers!" Droll pointed to the shoulder

of his crimson robes, now almost black with dried blood. "You see what the outside forces of evil have done!"

"Forgive me!" one of the flock screamed. Droll realized it must be the idiot who shot the gun. "I meant to smite evil with the bullet."

"You are not to blame." Droll did his best to smile directly at the idiot. "The evildoers who forced you to pick up that gun directed that bullet as surely as if they had pointed the trigger themselves! And that is what I have come to talk to you about tonight, my children. There are people out there who work against us—"

"No!" someone in the audience shouted.

"People who would destroy the Joke—"

"No!" half the audience screamed together. Droll had them now.

"Unless we destroy them first!" he shouted.

His flock went wild.

Droll raised his hands for silence. "You will recognize these evildoers when you see them, my children. For one wears the suit of a bat, and the other wears a pasty white face with a dark red smile so wide that it makes a mockery of the Joke!"

"Destroy!" someone in the audience shouted, and other members of the congregation took up the word as a chant. "Destroy! Destroy! Destroy!"

"Yes, we must destroy them now! And all of you, except for Larry and Tom, who will help me transport our collected wealth to someplace safe from these evildoers —all of you will go to the River Point Condominiums on Route 17 and smite them from the face of the earth!"

The Reverend Droll paused, and regarded all of his congregation. "Go forth, my children, and the Joke shall live forever!"

The crowd roared, then turned to carry out their holy master's order.

What a relief.

Now Droll would get out of here, with as much money as he could carry, and start a new life someplace else. Maybe he'd even start a new religion. His flock would kill The Joker; one less enemy Droll would have to worry about. Maybe he'd get lucky and they could get Batman, too. Of course, a lot of these idiots would probably die in the attempt, but what the hell, it would be that many less people to testify against him should he ever get caught.

Droll had to admit it. No matter how this turned out, he came out a winner.

There were no more electric shocks. The video images went on and on. It didn't matter. His reaction was always the same.

He'd learned what they wanted. He'd learned the only way to get through life.

Dick did nothing but laugh.

Dick was a real Joker.

27

"In here," George whispered. "You're going to protect me, now?"

"I'll do everything I can," Batman promised. "I never forget a favor."

They had traveled down to The Joker's lair using a circuitous route, starting in one of the half-finished buildings above, then descending one set of stairs, crawling some twenty feet through a large air duct, and descending a second staircase before flipping a switch and going back up a flight of stairs. Batman wondered for a bit if George was leading him into a trap, but decided that George was simply too scared. Besides, this was the sort of elaborate entrance that would appeal to someone like The Joker, a path where you seemed to double back and forth almost by whim.

It was such an elaborate puzzle to get into this place,

George told him, that The Joker never managed to keep much of a gang on hand. For one thing, the fewer people who knew the ins and outs of this place, the better it suited The Joker. To the best of George's knowledge, besides Samson and himself, there were only two others that spent any time down here—a Dr. Andrews and Big Mike. And George had heard that something had happened to Big Mike.

It took a good ten minutes for Batman and George to finally reach the heart of The Joker's hideout—an area that was once designated to be a "recreational sports complex." Once Batman was inside, his first job was to shut off all the traps and alarms so that the police could get in by a more direct path.

They hadn't seen any sign of life since they'd started through this maze, and there was no one in the inner hallway, either. Perhaps, for a change, The Joker's paranoia would work to Batman's advantage.

"Here it is," George said as he opened another door. "The control center."

Batman moved by the cowering Bernoff. The room was dominated by a wall covered by huge circuit breakers, dials, computer readouts, and one absurdly large lever. The Joker's touch again. This was the board George had told him about, and that lever was some sort of master switch.

Batman pulled the lever down, and was rewarded by a loud clank.

"So I've turned off all the alarms?" Batman asked.

George nodded. "And opened up every door besides. The Joker wanted to make sure he could get out of here in a hurry." He shuddered. "I imagine, though, that he'll stop by to see us first."

* * *

Batman looked up. The glass was gone. The cell door was open.

"Don't talk to me!" he shouted.

But nobody did. There was no one there.

The door had opened by itself. Batman was free.

"What was that noise?"

The Joker placed a reassuring hand on Andrews's shoulder. "There, there, Doctor. That little clank? That was just Batman's way of announcing himself."

"Batman? What are we going to do?"

"Well, we certainly won't panic. We need to go and see to our new 'Joker'." The original Joker clapped his hands. "You know, this is his coming-out party!"

Batman looked up. The glass was gone. The cell door was open.

"What?" Batman stood and stared. "Free?" He considered the implications.

"Free to walk, free to stroll, free to leave, that's my goal." He walked out of the cell. The corridor was empty. He snapped his fingers. This was all right.

"To fly like a bat is where it's at!"

Now where was that Joker?

The Joker laughed.

But there was another Joker in front of him.

"Ah," the second Joker said. "Are we looking in the mirror? Well, we certainly look good and ready. Yes, indeed. All ready to fight Batman!"

The Joker was going to fight Batman?

The Joker laughed.

* * *

Batman looked up. The glass was gone. The cell door was open.

Was this another one of The Joker's tricks? Well, this one would backfire on him. He'd smash The Joker on one of his own devices and grind him into small, bloody bits of pulp.

"To fly like a bat is where it's at!" someone called from the hall.

It had to be The Joker. Batman launched himself out into the hall to face his enemy.

He stopped dead. It wasn't The Joker. It was somebody else dressed like Batman.

He pushed the other man up against the wall. "All right. What's the meaning of this?"

The second man looked as startled as the first. "Uh. There's two. Won't do."

"Don't get smart with me!" the first Batman shouted. "I've wasted guys for less."

The other man shook his head. "Don't look now at what I see. There's not two of us, there's three."

The first Batman looked around. What was the guy talking about? Oh, hell. There was another guy dressed like Batman.

"What is this?" the first Batman muttered. "Some kind of farce?"

Gordon led a line of ten police cruisers into the River Point Condominium site. Someone else had gotten here before them. There must have been hundreds of them, mostly young, college-age kids, running around, shouting, smashing windows. It looked like they had a full-scale riot on their hands out here.

The commissioner spoke into his radio. "This is Gordon. I don't know what's going on here, men, but I suggest we proceed with caution. And I'm going to call in some backup."

Whatever this was, they had their hands full. For the time being, Batman was going to have to make it on his own.

There was no sign of The Joker yet. But Batman heard voices up ahead.

"Leave me alone! I don't want to deal with this!"

"It sure looks like too many cooks."

"Both of you'd better shut up before I put a fist through somebody's face!"

He couldn't believe what he saw when he turned the corner. There were three other men, more or less all dressed as Batman. Here were all the men The Joker had kidnapped and turned into—him.

"Oh, Lord!" the owner of the gruffest voice shouted. "Not another one!"

How should he handle this? As directly as possible was his guess. He kept on walking toward the other three. "What's the matter here?"

"What do you think is the matter?" the gruff-voiced one demanded. "We're lost? I've got two—no, now I've got three other people—who claim to be Batman."

Hmm. He had to be careful here. He had to consider how all these new batmen thought.

"But you know you're the real Batman," he said.

"Of course!" the gruff-voiced one replied. "But these two—"

"Also know they're the real Batman," he answered

for the other man. "As do I. But I don't think that matters."

"Why not?" another of the batmen asked in a shaky voice.

"Because one of us has to be the real Batman. And that one's going to catch The Joker."

"All right!" the Batman who hadn't spoken much shouted. "Let's fight!"

The real thing nodded his head pleasantly. "Let's all go after him, shall we?" He'd rather have these three with him than against him. He just hoped he could keep them from getting in the way.

Then he heard The Joker laugh.

The Joker was here somewhere. Batman had left George cowering back in the control room and headed for the noise.

He had run into a huge open space at the very center of the underground complex. Batman remembered seeing this space on the buildings' plans. Maybe, if they had ever finished this, it would have contained a basketball court or a swimming pool. Now it was just grey, immense, and empty.

"Batman," a familiar voice called from up above, "you're always dropping in so unexpectedly. And me without a thing to wear!"

Batman looked up to see five stories of windows and walkways above.

"So what's it to be," The Joker shouted. "The final showdown? Or should we make it the best two out of three?"

There was something wrong here. Even though he was

saying the right words, The Joker didn't sound the same. He looked different, too. There was something about his stance, though, that Batman recognized.

That wasn't really The Joker.

It was Dick.

28

Oh, this was too, too delightful.

The Joker looked down on his victim, poor, pitiful Batman, so far below, like an ant about to be squashed. But he looked so lonely down there, all alone in this big, big room. It was time to swing down and say hello, and maybe, just maybe, smash in the Batman's face.

He grabbed hold of the rope he had so handily provided for this very purpose. Ah, the man on the flying trapeze. So much space, so much freedom. Not like that church.

Church? What church? Who cared anything about church?

Where had that come from? Was The Joker going crazy?

It was Dick Grayson up there, wearing Joker makeup and a green wig. For some reason, though, he was acting like the real Joker, just as that fake Batman he'd met before believed he was the real thing. The Joker must be hypnotizing his victims somehow, clouding their minds to convince them that they were someone else.

Dick looked like he was going to grab that rope up there, swing down, and start fighting. Batman had to get through to him before someone got hurt.

"Dick!" he called.

"Di—ick?" the false Joker called back in a singsong. "Who? What? Sticks and stones can break my bones, but names can never hurt me."

Dick laughed as he grabbed the rope and swung toward Batman.

What could Batman do? Dick didn't know what he was doing. But Batman had no idea how deep this mind manipulation went. Once he got on the ground, he would have to expect his old partner to be every bit as deadly as the real Joker.

The laugh had given The Joker away. All four of them had run toward the sound. There, at the entrance to the cell blocks, they had found The Joker. And Dr. Andrews, too.

Batman frowned. How did he know about Dr. Andrews? It had something to do with needles. He couldn't think about it.

The Joker laughed. "Hoo-boy. Do we have company, or what?"

Dr. Andrews was not so cheerful. "But you don't understand." He hastily reached inside his lab coat. "They all believe they are Batman! They are dangerous!" When his hand reemerged, it held a gun.

"Doc," The Joker replied. "I wouldn't have it any other

way. Now, if you'll excuse me—" He turned and ran out of sight.

"I'm warning you," Andrews cautioned as he waved the gun back and forth. "Don't come any closer."

Someone had to deal with this. Batman guessed it had to be him.

"Get The Joker, boys!" he called to the other men in bat suits. Then he rushed the doctor.

Andrews tried to swing the gun around on the moving Batman. But the doctor wasn't as good with guns as he was with needles. Batman slammed the doctor's gun hand as the revolver went off, the bullet embedding itself in a nearby wall.

He jerked the gun out of Andrews's hand and floored the doctor with a single blow.

One problem gone. But now he had to finish things with The Joker.

"Banzai!" The Joker screamed as he launched himself through the air.

Batman leapt away from his swinging feet. Ah, well. He'd have to get him on the way back. He let go of the rope, did a smart somersault, and landed on his feet.

"Dick!" Batman yelled. Why did he keep calling him that. "That was you there, not The Joker. The Joker's nowhere near that athletic. That somersault was the sort of thing you used to do as Robin."

Robin? Why was he talking about Robin? Robin was dead! He had killed Robin. Just like he was going to kill Batman!

The Joker was filled with rage.

"I'll get you, bat-creep!" he screamed as he rushed his

opponent. He swung wildly, connecting with Batman's jaw. Robin was dead. He killed Robin. Robin was dead.

Batman socked him in the stomach.

"Dick!" Batman yelled again. Why was he calling him that? He wasn't Dick. Robin was dead. He swung at Batman again, but the batcreep easily sidestepped the blow. He had to concentrate. He wasn't Dick, was he? No, he was Robin. No, Robin was dead.

He was Nightwing.

He looked down at his fist. What was he doing? That was Batman.

Dick started to laugh.

And then he started to cry.

A high, spectral laugh floated down the corridor. The Joker was waiting for him, just ahead.

Once Dick had realized who he was, whatever they had done to him just seemed to fall away. Batman had left him to recover on the floor of the big central room, and gone after the real menace, the man who had killed Jason Todd. Dick should be able to take care of himself now, and Gordon would be along in a minute or two. It actually surprised Batman that it had taken the police commissioner this long to join them.

Batman walked down the corridor toward the confrontation he had been living for.

"Yoo-hoo!" a high, artificially feminine voice taunted him. "You still have to deal with me, sweetie pooh!"

Jason.

"Catch me if you cannnnn!"

Jason. Don't go.

Batman was walking down a row of small, open rooms,

all of which had been fitted with bars to make them into tiny cells.

The explosion.

There was no sign of The Joker. Only his voice leading Batman on.

"Just around the corner! Do you have to keep me waiting?"

Jason. No! Too late. Too late.

Batman saw a flash of white up ahead. He wanted this over with now.

He turned the corner and spotted The Joker's purple coat. He jumped for it.

Something clanged behind him.

Batman whirled around, The Joker's sportcoat in his hands. The coatless Joker waved at him from the other side of the bars.

"Have a nice stay!" The Joker called.

Batman realized he was locked in here.

"Not that you'll have long to think about it," The Joker continued as he walked into the cell opposite. He punched a panel out from the wall. Behind it was a large water pipe. "Batman's going for a little swim. We are underground, of course. And this wing has no drainage at all. It will be such a shame when the water fills it up entirely, won't it?"

Batman didn't believe this. He had been so obsessed with the death of his former partner, he'd walked right into one of The Joker's traps.

There might be some way he could get out of this. The acid capsules in his utility belt could eat away at the bars, and perhaps weaken them enough for him to kick them out. But The Joker would get away.

The Joker twisted a large faucet as he leapt out of the way. Water rushed out of an opening the size of a basketball.

"Now, if you'll excuse me, Batman, I have to open a couple more of these down the corridor. I never was very good at conserving water." He chuckled. "As you drown, please think of me."

"You're not going anywhere, Joker," another voice said.

"What?" The Joker screamed in disbelief. "You can't be out here." He pointed at Batman. "You're in there!"

He had found The Joker at last.

"No!" the white-faced trickster shouted. "I refuse to believe this!"

Batman realized The Joker had one of his look-alikes trapped behind bars. Well, The Joker was dealing with the real Batman now. He moved as quickly as he could through the foot of water flooding the floor.

"This is not happening! Do you want to make The Joker crazy?" He pulled an ornate revolver from his pants. "One of you will have to go!"

He had to stop The Joker now. But what could he do against a gun? For some reason he wasn't wearing his utility belt. He had only his wits to rely on.

He remembered something about these cells.

"Watch out, Joker!" he shouted as he kicked the other man back against the bars with his boots—insulated boots with rubber soles.

He slammed his fist into a large red button by the side of the cell.

There was a crack like lightning as The Joker screamed,

electricity pulsing through his body as it formed a circuit from the bars to the water below. The villain fell forward as the electrical system shorted out, leaving half the cell block in darkness.

Batman had only meant to incapacitate his foe. Even in the semidark, he could tell The Joker was dead.

Being Batman was serious business.

The other Batman turned off the water, then pressed another button outside the real Batman's cell. The cell door popped open.

"Thanks," the real Batman said as he walked out to meet his double. "You seem to know a lot about this place."

The other Batman thought about this. "Yes, I do, don't I?"

"You'd only know it if you'd spent some time down here," Batman mentioned.

"What are you implying?"

Batman answered the other man's question with one of his own. "Does the name Steven Winter mean anything to you?"

The other man got a very confused look on the lower half of his face. "Winter? Could be."

"Don't get me wrong," Batman continued. "I think you make a very good Batman." Maybe, he thought, there's a lot of Batman in other people. And thinking of the way Jason's death had consumed him so, maybe there were a lot of other people in Batman as well.

He walked over to take a closer look at The Joker.

Except when he got nearer to the man and saw his smeared clown makeup, he realized it wasn't The Joker after all.

"Oops!" a mocking voice called from farther down into the cell block. "Did bat-boy make a booboo?"

Both batmen turned.

"The Joker!" they said together.

They were answered by an eerie, fading laugh.

Dick Grayson sat in the large featureless room, waiting for a reason to get up. He had been through so much. But, thanks in large part to Batman, he knew who he was again. He was Dick Grayson, and he was Nightwing. But he was more than that. There was a part of him that would always be Robin, too; the young man at Batman's side.

Perhaps, on some level, this was something he had always known. When he finally got a chance to mull this over, he might know more about himself than he ever had before.

All this thought wasn't getting him off the bare cement floor. It was time for Dick Grayson and Nightwing and the former Robin to pull themselves together.

He heard an all-too-familiar laugh.

The Joker! Dick looked around the room as if he were seeing it for the first time. The place had a floor the size of a high school gym, but the walls rose a good half-dozen stories above him, as if this was intended as an open courtyard. The Joker's voice had come from somewhere in front of him, but was it from this basement level, or one of the floors above?

Dick stood and turned, searching for a hiding place. He saw an alcove on the far side of the room, which led to a doorway hidden in shadow. He ran to the darkened space as quietly as he could. If The Joker was coming this way, Dick wanted the element of surprise.

He flattened his back against the shadowed wall, and realized he wasn't even breathing hard. There was something about The Joker's laugh that had given him back his energy, and his sense of purpose. He guessed he was more like Batman in that respect than he had thought.

Everybody that Dick had ever been, and everybody he was now, was ready for this fight.

He had to stop The Joker. But he realized, with this other Batman running by his side, that he wasn't going to do it alone. And Batman realized that was exactly the way to do it.

The plan formed in his mind as they hurried down the corridor. The Joker had always liked puzzles, word plays, mind games, anything to link his crimes together. For The Joker, it wasn't enough to steal. He had to link his crimes together to make them interesting, and the games he devised to join his crimes had become deadlier over the years. Nothing, however, was deadlier than his newfound use of psychology.

But maybe they could use this same psychology to their advantage.

The Joker's laugh drifted back to them again from somewhere up ahead. This could easily be another trap. Batman, however, planned to turn the trap around.

He motioned for the man with him to stop. Farther down the corridor he could see another open doorway, which led again to that large central courtyard. Batman knew, from studying the map back at City Hall, that almost every one of the hallways in the underground complex led back to this central area. But his knowledge was far too general. The Joker knew every one of these corridors, along with all the new adjustments The Joker might have made; adjustments that wouldn't have shown up in those plans at City Hall.

"This is where we're going to have our showdown with The Joker," Batman explained in a soft voice. "Both of us. And forget what I said about you being Steven Winter. For now, you are the Batman."

"And you?" asked the Batman who was no longer Winter.

"Oh, I'm Batman, too. That's the only way my plan can work. Once we reach the door, I'll go left, you go right. We have to move fast when we get in there. And stay close to the wall—it makes you less of an obvious target. I believe we can depend on The Joker to do the rest."

Almost as an afterthought, he added, "Oh, and I'll give you a couple lines to memorize."

Dick saw not one, but two batmen run into the room. Each one sprinted toward an opposite corner. And, somewhere overhead, he heard The Joker laugh.

"Now!" the Batman to the right yelled. Both costumed men stopped and turned away from Dick to look up in the direction of the merriment. Dick looked up, too, and saw The Joker, sitting in a window one story up. He had a large pipe on his shoulder—it was a bazooka.

"Oh, dear!" The Joker called. "An embarrassment of riches! Too many batmen!" He patted the weapon on his shoulder. "And I can only blow one of you to kingdom come."

"Which one will it be, Joker?" asked the Batman on the left in a growl that altered his real voice.

"I think the one with the utility belt—" The Joker frowned. "Where's the utility belt?"

"Well, it isn't fair if everyone can't have one," the Batman on the left replied in a voice an octave too low.

"All for one and one for all," the other costumed hero added in that same growl. "That's the Batman motto."

Dick saw what Batman was doing. The Joker couldn't act if he couldn't determine the proper target. At least Dick knew which one was real; at least he thought he did. Batman was even consciously adjusting his stance so that his body language was a little different.

The Joker giggled. "So I blow one of you away, then disappear and reload."

The Joker wasn't confused enough. Maybe it was time for another Joker to step in.

Dick laughed. "Wait a minute! Who's this stealing my thunder?"

He stepped out of the shadows.

The Joker glared down at him. "Don't mess with me, boy! I made you what you are today."

"What?" Dick called out with melodramatic indignation. "The Joker is a self-made man."

"I'll say," the real Joker replied. "And one of a kind." He swung the bazooka around to point at Dick.

"This looks like a job for Batman!" the costumed hero on the left shouted.

"And Batman is here!" added the hero on the right.

Dick saw they both had Batarangs in their hands, each with an attached line. They were going to try and hogtie The Joker.

"Wait a moment!" the real Joker yelled. "I know this game!"

The Joker was getting on top of this again. That would never do.

"I'll say!" Dick shouted in turn. "Let's attack someone important around here, like me!"

"I can't take this anymore!" the real Joker announced. "I'm going to blow all of you away—with grenades!"

But there was a chorus of shouts before The Joker could move back toward his private weapons stash.

"There he is!" one voice yelled.

"Now we'll see who the real Batman is around here!" another added.

"One's a hero, the rest are zero!" a third voice chimed in. Dick could see three men in Batman costumes running on the other side of the windows of The Joker's floor.

The Batman on Dick's right—the real Batman, he guessed—threw his bat-shaped boomerang. The attached nylon cord caught The Joker's bazooka as the Batarang spun around the pipe. Batman yanked the other end of the cord, pulling the weapon out of the startled Joker's grip. The boomerang clattered to the floor.

The Joker screeched and ran.

Dick walked forward to meet the two costumed heroes. "All right!" he called. "Who's the real Batman here?"

The man on the right turned and smiled. "Maybe," he said, "there's a little of Batman in all of us."

"I'll agree to that," his partner on the left added. "Now let's go get The Joker."

The police had had their hands full for a few minutes, but they had finally rounded up most of the mob. They all seemed to be members of the Church of Perpetual Happiness. They were not shy in the least about mentioning this fact, nor the fact that they had been sent to destroy

The Joker. Gordon thought they had collected more than a few candidates for psychiatric examination here. He imagined, since he had just arrested the entire congregation, that this might be the beginning of the end for the church as well, especially since a couple of his detectives had just called in to inform Gordon that they had apprehended Droll along with some tens of millions of dollars in cash.

Now that they had the situation in hand here, they had to see what they could do about helping Batman.

"Get away from me!"

What now? The scream had come from the entryway to one of the half-finished condominium buildings. At first, Gordon thought it was one of the few church members they hadn't managed to round up.

But then he saw it was The Joker.

"Get back! I'm warning you!"

"Who cares?" another voice replied. "I just want this over with." Batman stepped out of the shadows.

And then a second Batman followed. "We do The Joker in, and then we win."

And then a third. "We all want a piece of you, Joker. What say we divide you into thirds? Big, bloody thirds."

"You don't understand!" The Joker wailed, real desperation in his voice. "You're not real! I created you!"

"Not real?" shouted the last Batman to speak. "This isn't real?" All three men in Batman costumes jumped on The Joker.

"The Joker?" someone else yelled. "Get The Joker!"

The half-dozen members of the church that Gordon's men hadn't captured all ran toward the fight.

Oh, no. Whatever was going on here, the police had to put an end to it once and for all.

*   *   *

"And what happened?" Batman asked in disbelief.

"When we got over to the pile of bodies, The Joker was gone," Gordon explained. "But not very far away. My men saw him fleeing the scene in a purple Dodge. We have four cruisers in close pursuit. We'll get him."

Would they? Batman hoped so. For now, they had to pick up the pieces. Batman hid Dick away from the police in the Batmobile. Both Dick and Steve Winter seemed confused, but on the way to recovery. Batman imagined it would be the same for the other three men who had been dressed up as him. Both Dr. Andrews and Reverend Droll were in custody, and George identified the dead Joker as his fellow gang member Samson before George, too, was taken off to jail.

And Batman had seen part of himself, too. When Dick was feeling better, they really would have to talk. And Batman had to realize that Jason *was* dead. He had to put the anger, and the hurt, behind him. They had no place in him when he was fighting crime.

Which only left The Joker. Gordon swore his men would capture Batman's old foe. Batman wasn't so sure, but he did know one thing, now that The Joker had shown himself again.

One way or another, Batman swore, The Joker was his.